The Forest Woman

The Forest Woman

Bankim Chandra Chatterjee

Translated by Radha Chakravarty

Hesperus Worldwide

Hesperus Worldwide
Published by Hesperus Press Limited
19 Bulstrode Street, London W1U 2JN
www.hesperuspress.com

First published in Bengali as *Kapalkundala* in 1866
This translation first published in *The Bankimchandra Omnibus Vol 1*,
Penguin India, 2005
First published by Hesperus Press Limited, 2011

English language translation © Radha Chakravarty, 2005
Introduction © Radha Chakravarty, 2011

Designed and typeset by Fraser Muggeridge studio
Printed in Jordan by Jordan National Press

ISBN: 978-1-84391-851-6

Contents

Introduction

'If a woman is brought up from infancy to the age of sixteen
by a Kapalik in a forest on the seacoast, and if she knows
no man except the ascetic, knows nothing of society and
roams the forest alone, how far will she change if married
and brought into society? Can the Kapalik's influence on
her disappear altogether?'

When Bankim Chandra Chatterjee (1838–1894) posed this
hypothetical question to friends and family, he was told that such
a woman, though initially alienated, would eventually adapt to
societal expectations and learn to love her husband and children.
Bankim was clearly not satisfied with this reply, for his second
Bengali novel *Kapalkundala* (1866), here published under the
title *The Forest Woman*, he created an extraordinary female
protagonist through whom he could explore his own answer to
this question.

The publication of *The Forest Woman* took the Kolkata
literary world by storm, and confirmed Bankim Chandra's repu-
tation as one of the pioneers of the Indian novel. Readers
were captivated by this dark, haunting tale of a stranded
traveller's ill-starred love for a beautiful woman he encounters
in a forest on a desolate seashore. Together, Nabokumar and
Kapalkundala escape the clutches of a kapalik, an ascetic bent
on human sacrifice. Nabokumar marries Kapalkundala and
brings her back to his village home, but discovers that this child
of nature, a foundling brought up in the wilds by a kapalik
who practises esoteric tantric rituals, feels like a misfit in her
husband's social and domestic world. The plot thickens with
the appearance of the seductive Motibibi, a fugitive from the
Mughal emperor's court who develops an amorous interest in
Nabokumar. Motibibi's intrigue and the kapalik's relentless

pursuit of Kapalkundala drive the narrative swiftly and inexorably to its tragic denouement.

The story is set in the early seventeenth century, when the Mughals, having subjugated the Afghans, were trying to consolidate their hold over the newly acquired province of Bengal, and the Portuguese had begun to make inroads into the local maritime scene. Bankim probably drew upon the same historical sources that he had used for his first novel, *Durgeshnandini*: Charles Stewart's history of Bengal (1813), and Alexander Dow's translation of Farishta's *Tarikh-e-Jahangiri*, from the three-volume *History of Hindostan* (1768). Literary inspiration came from multiple sources, including Sanskrit classical drama, medieval Bengali literature, the plays of Shakespeare and the historical romances of Walter Scott. Kapalkundala's name recalls the protagonist of the ancient Sanskrit text *Malatimadhava*, and her character is often compared to Kalidasa's Shakuntala and Shakespeare's Miranda. The kapalik in the novel is probably drawn from life, for in 1860, while serving in the Midnapore district in Bengal, Bankim had been shadowed by a tantric who dwelt in a dense forest facing the sea near Chandpur.

While using a historical framework, however, Bankim often takes liberties with factual details. Scholars point out, for instance, that Mehrunnissa's father, Mirza Ghiyas Tahrani, received a title from Jahangir, not Akbar, and that her first husband was named Sher Afkan Ali, not Sher Afghan as in the novel. Bankim's protagonists are not eminent historical figures, but people whose lives are far removed from the public glare of history. Even Motibibi, an aspirant to the Emperor's hand, eventually leaves the court and returns to the private realm.

Bankim was a staunch patriot, best remembered today as the composer of 'Vande Mataram', the song that became the nationalist anthem against colonial rule. His choice of a historical theme in *The Forest Woman* may have been inspired not only by literary sources, but also by a nationalist desire to reclaim India's precolonial past. He may have also found it more expedient to set the story of Nabokumar's love for Kapalkundala in an earlier period, because the idea of premarital romantic love did not match the conventions of his own times. In nineteenth-century Bengal, the system of arranged marriage ensured that girls were married off at a very young age to men selected by their families, precluding the likelihood of romance before marriage. *The Forest Woman* was written at a time when Bengal was riven by disputes among the intelligentsia about the need for social change, centred upon the position of women. While the liberal reformists argued in favour of women's education, widow remarriage and abolition of child marriage and sati, the conservatives clung strongly to their traditions, to protect the purity of Hindu culture from the 'corrupting' influence of western mores. The novel form provided a space where these debates could be played out through fictional characters and situations.

Though Bankim writes of a bygone era, the authorial sensibility that emerges from the narrative is not backward-looking, but in some ways remarkably modern. Nabokumar, as his name suggests, represents the 'New Man', braver than the fellow travellers who abandon him, sceptical about religious ritual, open to the idea of marrying for love, and tenderly tolerant of Kapalkundala's unconventional behaviour until his mind is poisoned by jealousy. His love is one-sided, though. Unlike her literary precursors, Shakespeare's Miranda and Kalidasa's Shakuntala, Kapalkundala remains incapable of human attachments, for she is as indifferent and self-sufficient as Nature itself: 'love is the primary strand in the ties that bind us to life. Kapalkundala did not have such ties – she had no ties at all' (p. 109). From the position of an outsider, Kapalkundala questions the repressive social norms that judge a woman by her external acts alone. When Shyamasundari tries to dissuade her from going out into the woods at night, she protests,

> 'What's the harm? Do you, too, believe that the simple act of going out at night will make a loose woman of me?'
> 'I don't believe that. But wicked people will say wicked things.'
> 'Let them say what they will. That won't make me a wicked person… Had I known that marriage, for a woman, means slavery, I would never have married at all.'
>
> (p. 87)

She sees no harm in her nocturnal rendezvous with a stranger:

> She was sure that such a meeting was harmless, unless intended for a wrongful purpose. Just as persons of the same sex had the right to meet each other, so also, she felt, should persons of the opposite sexes enjoy the mutual right to intermingle.
>
> (p. 95)

Kapalkundala displays an individualism here that is strikingly modern. Bankim uses his asocial protagonist to critique the narrow-mindedness of caste Hindu society.

Kapalkundala's innocence also contrasts starkly with the worldliness of Lutfunnissa, who belongs to the larger realm of politics, beyond the narrow sphere of provincial Hindu-Bengali society. The Mughal emperor's court in Agra is a centre of pomp, wealth, power, corruption and intrigue. Thwarted in her ambitions of becoming empress, Lutfunnissa leaves the imperial court and returns to Bengal as Motibibi. Straddling the separate worlds of provincial Bengal and imperial Agra, the figure of this alluring, complex woman demonstrates the impact of history on the lives of ordinary people.

A strong sense of fate hangs over the entire narrative. Omens and portents foreshadow the tragic ending. Kapalkundala herself seems like an embodiment of blind Fate; Nabokumar's infatuation with her leads him to his doom, but she remains utterly indifferent to the destruction she brings in her wake. The first edition of *The Forest Woman* featured a less tragic conclusion but in subsequent editions, Bankim replaced this ending with a conclusion more appropriate to the mood and atmosphere of the novel. Yet the plot is not driven by fantasy or the supernatural; the events unfold according to their own internal logic, and the motives and actions of the characters are explicable in realistic terms.

Bankim's mastery of the art of storytelling is evident not only in the seamless design of the plot, but also in the brilliance of his prose style. An unusual feature of this text is the use of epigraphs before every chapter. Drawn from a wide-ranging, eclectic mix of European, Sanskrit and Bengali texts, the epigraphs invite the reader to recognise this novel's links with multiple literary traditions. Bankim's ability to integrate indigenous and European influences highlights the literary and cultural encounters that triggered the emergence of 'modern' Indian literature.

Bankim Chandra remains controversial for his alleged Hindu orthodoxy and the anti-Muslim stance of some of his later writings. In *The Forest Woman*, though, Hindu–Muslim conflicts do not occupy centre stage. If the Mughal court is represented as a den of deception and intrigue, so is the kapalik's version of ritualistic Tantric Hinduism rejected as destructive and bloodthirsty. Instead of championing the cause of any particular faith or community, the text dramatises the power of impersonal, amoral forces such as nature, destiny and history, which shape the course of human lives and relationships.

The Forest Woman has been translated into several Indian languages, and adapted for the stage and screen. There have also been attempts to retell the story from different perspectives. Sayyed Abn-al-Hussain's retelling (1922), for instance, parodies the text by presenting Kapalkundala, rather than Lutfunnissa, as the 'corrupt' woman, while Damodar Mukherjee's sequel, titled *Mrinmayi* (1874), replaces the original ending with a happy one. The first English translation of *The Forest Woman* by H.A.D. Philips of the Bengal Judicial Service appeared in London in 1885. This was followed by D.N. Ghosh's translation, published in Kolkata in 1919, and more recently, by Gautam Chakravarty's translation, published in Delhi in 2005. Bankim revised *The Forest Woman* through eight editions in his lifetime, the last in 1891. Apart from the altered ending, he made one other important modification, deleting an entire chapter comprising a short meditation on fate and free will. The present translation is based on the final edition of *The Forest Woman*. To evoke for today's readers the ethos of a bygone age, to capture the flavour of Bankim's prose without sacrificing lucidity and readability, and to make this text accessible to readers unfamiliar with the language and historical-cultural-literary context of the original, has proved a challenge as difficult as it was inspiring.

– *Radha Chakravarty, 2011*

The Forest Woman

Part 1

At the Estuary

Floating straight obedient to the stream.
Comedy of Errors

About two hundred and fifty years ago, late one night in the month of Magh, a passenger boat was on its way back from Gangasagar. It was customary those days for passenger boats to travel together in groups, to protect themselves from the Portuguese and other pirates. But this boat was unaccompanied, because in the dense fog that had enveloped the horizon in the early hours, the sailors, losing their orientation, had steered the vessel away from the rest of the fleet. Now they had no idea where they were headed, or in which direction. Many of the passengers were asleep. Only two men remained awake: one was old, the other young. They were engaged in conversation.

'How far can we travel tonight?' the old man broke off to enquire of the sailors.

'I couldn't say,' replied the oarsman, after some hesitation.

Enraged, the old man began to rant at the oarsman.

'Sir, when matters are in God's hands, even learned men cannot predict what might transpire,' the young man intervened. 'How can this illiterate man say anything for certain? Please don't agitate yourself.'

'Not be agitated?' exclaimed the old man sharply. 'How is that possible, when rascally robbers have snatched away the paddy from twenty to twenty-five acres of my land? What will my children survive on, all year?'

He had received these tidings after he was already at the estuary, from travellers who arrived there subsequently.

'I did point out earlier that it was not a good idea for Sir to have come on this pilgrimage, because his household has no other guardian,' the young man reminded him.

'Not come on this pilgrimage?' exclaimed the old man as sharply as before. 'With three-quarters of my lifespan over already? When should I build my store of virtue for the life to come, if not at this stage?'

'If I understand the scriptures correctly,' observed the young man, 'it's possible to prepare for the afterlife in one's own home, just as well as on a pilgrimage.'

'Then why did you undertake this journey?' the old man demanded.

'As I've said before, I had a great desire to see the ocean,' replied the young man. 'That is why I came here.'

'Ah! What a vision!' he mused, in a softer voice. 'Never to be forgotten in all eternity!' In Sanskrit, he quoted,

Behold the remote blue shore, densely encircled by tal and tamal!
And there, like a long, dark stain, stretch the salt waters of the deep.

The old man paid no attention to the poetry. He was listening with rapt attention to the conversation of the sailors.

'O bhai, my brother! What a terrible thing we've done!' one sailor was saying to another. 'Are we now in the open seas? Or are we approaching some unknown land? I couldn't say!'

The speaker sounded very frightened. The old man realised that there was cause for anxiety.

'What's the matter?' he asked the oarsman, fearfully.

The oarsman made no reply. But the young man stepped out on deck without waiting for an answer. He found that it was almost dawn. The world, all around, was enveloped in dense fog; sky, stars, moon, shore, nothing could be seen. He realised that the sailors had lost their way. Unable to ascertain the direction in which they were going, they were terrified of drowning in the open seas.

The passengers within the boat had remained unaware of all this, because of a screen draped over the front of the cabin, to protect them from the cold. But the young traveller understood their predicament, and explained it to the old man. This caused a huge commotion on board. Some of the female passengers, aroused from slumber by the sound of voices, began to scream as soon as they heard the news.

'To the shore! To the shore! To the shore!' cried the old man.

'If we knew where the shore was, would we be in such grave danger?' asked the young man, with a faint smile.

At this, the passengers began to scream even more loudly. The young traveller somehow managed to calm them down.

'There's no cause for anxiety,' he assured the sailors. 'Day has broken. In a few hours, the sun will be up. The boat will certainly not be destroyed in two or three hours. Stop rowing now, and let the boat drift with the current. Later, once the sun comes up, we can discuss what is to be done.'

The sailors accepted his advice and proceeded accordingly.

For a long time, the sailors sat idle. The passengers were half-dead with fright. There was not much of a breeze, so they could not really sense the undulation of the waves. All the same, everyone assumed that death was close at hand. The men began to silently chant goddess Durga's name, the women wailed in many voices. Only one woman did not weep: she had sacrificed her child to the waters of the Gangasagar estuary, having failed to lift him out of the water after the holy dip.

They waited until morning seemed close at hand. Suddenly, the sailors created a great uproar, calling upon the five pirs of the ocean.

'What is it? What is it? Tell us, oarsman, what has happened?' cried the passengers.

'The sun is up! The sun is up! Land ahoy!' cried the oarsman, amidst a babble of voices.

All the passengers came out on deck, curious to see where they had arrived, and to ascertain the truth about their predicament. They found that the sun was up. The air was now completely clear of the fog's shadow. The day was well advanced. The boat had not drifted out into the open seas, but had merely reached the river's mouth. At this point, though, the river was at its widest. On one side, the shore was very close to the boat, indeed – in fact, within about thirty feet of it; but the opposite shore could not be seen at all. In every direction, wherever one looked, there stretched a vast expanse of water, sparkling in the playful sunshine, extending to the horizon, where it merged with the sky. The water, seen at close range, had a river's usual muddy hue, but acquired a bluish gleam where it stretched into the distance. The passengers concluded with certainty that they had reached the high seas; but they counted themselves fortunate that, due to the proximity of the beach, they had no cause for anxiety. They determined their orientation from the position of the sun. The stretch of land facing them was readily identified as the western shore of the sea. Along the beach, not far from the boat, was the mouth of a river, flowing gently into the sea like a stream of gold. To the right of the estuary, countless birds of all varieties could be seen, frolicking on the wide stretch of sand. This river is today known as the Rasulpur.

On the Beach

Ingratitude! Thou marble-hearted friend!
King Lear

When the passengers' excited babble had subsided, the sailors proposed that, while high tide was still far away, they could cook their meal on the beach facing them. Afterwards, as soon as the tide came in, they could proceed on their homeward journey. The passengers accepted this suggestion. Once the sailors had brought the boat to the shore, the travellers alighted, and busied themselves with their daily ablutions.

Ablutions completed, when they began preparations for cooking, another difficulty presented itself: there was no firewood on board. For fear of tigers, nobody was willing to fetch firewood from the embankment above. Ultimately, realising they would all starve, the old man addressed the young man we have spoken of earlier:

'Nabokumar, my son! If you don't tackle the situation, all of us will die.'

'Very well, I shall go,' decided Nabokumar, after a brief hesitation. 'I need an axe, and someone to accompany me with a da – a chopping blade.'

Nobody was willing to accompany Nabokumar.

'When it's time to eat, we'll see who joins me,' remarked Nabokumar. Girding his waist, he picked up the axe and set off alone in search of firewood.

Clambering up the embankment, Nabokumar found no trace of human habitation, anywhere within sight. Only forests were to be seen, not graced with rows of giant trees, nor densely wooded, but consisting instead of clusters of small shrubs, covering the land in patches. Unable to spot any firewood worth collecting, Nabokumar had to walk far inland, away from the riverbank, in search of suitable trees. Finally, having located a tree that would suit his purpose, he gathered all the wood he required. He found the load very difficult to carry. As he was not a poor man's son, Nabokumar was unaccustomed to such chores; having gone in search of firewood without considering the consequences, he now found his load very burdensome. All the same, having once taken on a task, it was not in

Nabokumar's nature to give up easily; so he began to somehow stagger back with his burden of firewood. He would go a little way, then sit and rest awhile, before moving on again, making his way back in this fashion.

Nabokumar's return was thus delayed. Meanwhile, his companions grew anxious, fearing that Nabokumar had been killed by a tiger. After a reasonable time had elapsed, they were convinced in their hearts that this was indeed what had happened. Yet, no one had the courage to climb the embankment and advance inland in search of him.

While the travellers speculated thus, a tumult broke out in the waters. The sailors realised that the tide had turned. They were well aware that, in such places, the waves at high tide buffet the shore so violently, that any boats or other river craft that happen to be within range are smashed to bits. So, they rapidly untied the boat and began to row away towards the middle of the river. No sooner had the boat moved away, than the stretch of sand before them was inundated with water. The terrified travellers had barely managed to scramble on board; the rice, with all other items placed on the beach, was swept away in the tide. Unfortunately, the sailors, lacking expertise, could not control the boat, which was carried by the torrent, out into the middle of the Rasulpur River.

'But we've left Nabokumar behind!' cried one of the passengers.

'Oh, as if your Nabokumar is still alive!' scoffed a sailor. 'He has been devoured by jackals.'

The force of the tide was carrying the boat midstream, far out into the Rasulpur River. It would be difficult to steer it back. The sailors struggled with all their might to pull out of the current. Even in the cold month of Magh, the sweat began to pour down their foreheads. With incredible effort, they managed to pull out of Rasulpur River, but as soon as the boat emerged into the open waters, it encountered even stronger currents which spun the vessel around, propelling it northwards with the speed of an arrow. The sailors could not control its movements at all. The boat did not return.

When the tide subsided sufficiently for the vessel's speed to be brought under control, they had travelled far beyond the mouth of the Rasulpur. They now had to decide whether or not it would be possible to return in search of Nabokumar. It must be mentioned at this juncture that Nabokumar's fellow-travellers were merely his neighbours, not his close friends. After considering the situation, they concluded that to turn back from their present position meant waiting for the tide to ebb again. Night would descend after that, making navigation impossible; they would have to await the next day's high tide. Until then, all of them would starve. Two days without food would bring them close to death. Besides, the sailors were unwilling to turn back; they were not under the passengers' command. The sailors insisted that Nabokumar had been killed by tigers. That was the likeliest possibility. So, why inflict such suffering on themselves?

Considering all this, the travellers thought it wise to proceed on their homeward journey without Nabokumar, who was left to survive somehow on that dreadful seashore.

If someone, hearing this account, should vow never to fetch firewood for others who are starving, such a person deserves to be ridiculed. Those naturally predisposed to banish their benefactor to the forest, will always do so. But one naturally predisposed to fetch firewood for others, will continue to do so, even if repeatedly banished to the forest. Why should someone else's ignoble nature deter one from aspiring to nobility?

In the Wilderness

Life's a veil
Which if withdrawn, would but disclose the frown
Of one who hates us, so the night was shown
And grimly darkled o'er their faces pale
And hopeless eyes.
Don Juan

Not far from the spot where the travellers had abandoned Nabokumar, two tiny villages, named Daulatpur and Dariapur, have now appeared. But during the period in question, there was no trace of human habitation in that area, which was a complete wilderness. But unlike other parts of Bengal, the land in this region was not flat and free of undulations. For several miles, from the mouth of the Rasulpur to the Subarnarekha, stretches an unbroken chain of sand hills. If they were slightly higher, these hillocks could have been described as a low, sandy mountain-range. Today, people call them sand dunes. Viewed from afar, the white crests of these dunes shine gloriously in the afternoon sunlight. No tall trees grow there. The sand dunes are scantily wooded at the base, but their middle and upper areas shine with a stark, white beauty, free of any shade. The vegetation covering the base of the sand dunes consists mainly of scrub, wild tamarisk and wildflowers.

In this cheerless place, Nabokumar had been abandoned by his companions. Returning to the riverbank with his load of firewood, he could not see the boat. He felt a sudden, wild surge of terror, but did not imagine that his fellow-travellers had permanently deserted him. Convinced that they had moved the boat to some nearby protected spot when the beach was flooded at high tide, he was sure they would soon seek him out. In this expectation, he lingered for a while on the sandy shore, waiting for the boat, but it did not return. Nor did any of the passengers reappear. Nabokumar was famished. Unable to wait any longer, he scoured the shores of the river for the boat. Finding no trace of it anywhere, he returned to the original spot. The boat still nowhere in sight, he concluded that it must have been carried away at high tide, and that his fellow-travellers, on their way back to fetch him, were taking a long time to row against the current. But even the tide receded. Now he was convinced the boat, unable to turn back against the force of the tide, was surely coming back for him now, at ebb-tide. But the tide continued to ebb, the day wore on, and eventually, it was sunset. If the boat was going to return, it should have done so by now.

Then it dawned on Nabokumar that either the rough waves at high tide had caused the boat to sink, or else his companions had abandoned him in this desolate place.

There was no village in sight, no refuge, no signs of human life, nor any food or drink; the river-water was unbearably salty, but he was wracked by hunger and thirst. There was no place to shelter from the cold, nor a warm wrap to shield his body. Without refuge, without any protective clothing, he would have to sleep under the open sky, exposed to the dampness of the falling dew, on this ice-cold, windswept riverbank. At night, he was likely to chance upon a beast of prey. Death seemed inevitable.

Nabokumar was too agitated to remain in one place for long. Abandoning the shore, he clambered up the embankment and began to roam about aimlessly. Night descended. In the moisture-laden sky, the silent stars appeared, exactly as in Nabokumar's own home country. Darkness enveloped this desolate place. Earth, sky and sea were utterly silent: only the roar of the ocean could be heard, and occasionally, the call of some wild beast. Still, Nabokumar wandered among the sand dunes, under that dark, chilly sky. He meandered in the valleys and plateaus, at the foot of the sand hills and across their crests.

At every step, he could have been attacked by some beast of prey. But to remain in one fixed spot would expose him to the same danger.

As he wandered about, Nabokumar began to feel exhausted, the more so for having gone without food all day. He rested against a sand dune. His warm, cosy bed at home came to mind. In a state of physical and mental exhaustion, one's thoughts are sometimes overcome by drowsiness. Lost in thought, Nabokumar drifted off to sleep. But for this law of human nature, the unchecked flood of our worldly troubles would often seem too much for us to tolerate.

On the Crest of the Sand Dune

He beheld in surprise, not far away, a vision that filled him with dread.
Meghnadbadh

The night was far advanced when Nabokumar awakened from his slumber. He was amazed to find himself still alive, not yet devoured by tigers. He looked around for approaching tigers. Far ahead, in the distance, he suddenly spotted a light. To make sure his eyes were not deluding him, he gazed at the light with full concentration. Gradually, the light seemed to grow larger and brighter; he was convinced it was the glow of a fire. The realisation instantly revived Nabokumar's hopes of survival. The glow could only signal the presence of some human habitation, for this was not the season for forest fires. Rising to his feet, Nabokumar raced towards the light.

'Is this a ghostly light?' he wondered, for a moment. 'It might be. But if daunted by fear, how can we protect our lives?'

Having arrived at this conclusion, he advanced fearlessly

towards the light, obstructed at every step by trees, creepers and mounds of sand. Trampling upon the undergrowth, stepping over sand-heaps, Nabokumar forged ahead. Nearing the light's source, he saw a fire burning on the crest of a sand dune, and revealed by its glow, silhouetted against the sky, a seated human form. Determined to approach this man on the sand dune's crest, Nabokumar proceeded without slowing his pace. He began to ascend the slope. He felt some pangs of anxiety now, but continued his ascent with unfaltering firmness of tread. What he saw when he came face to face with the man on the crest of the mound, made his hair stand on end. He could not decide whether to stay, or to retreat.

Eyes closed, the man seemed lost in meditation. At first, he did not see Nabokumar. Inspecting his appearance, Nabokumar surmised that he must be about fifty years old. He could see no clothing on the man's body, which was wrapped in leopard-skin from waist to knee. On his neck, the man wore a string of rudraksha beads, and his broad countenance was framed by dense, tangled locks of hair. Before him was a heap of burning logs, whose glow had guided Nabokumar to that spot. A terrible stench assailed Nabokumar's nostrils, and glancing at the place occupied by the stranger, he could sense its source. The man with the coiling locks was seated on a rotting, headless corpse. Nabokumar was even more terrified when he saw, placed before the meditating figure, a human skull containing a crimson fluid. Scattered all around were human bones; in fact, even the beads of the rudraksha necklace were interspersed with tiny bits of bone. Nabokumar stared at the scene, transfixed. He was in two minds whether to advance or to abandon the spot. He had heard of kapaliks, followers of the ascetic cult of goddess Kali. This man, he realised, was a member of that dreaded sect.

When Nabokumar arrived at the spot, the kapalik, immersed in holy ritual, prayer or meditation, took no notice of the young man.

'Who are you?' he asked in Sanskrit, after a long time.

'A Brahmin,' replied Nabokumar.

'Wait,' instructed the kapalik, and busied himself with the same rituals as before. Nabokumar remained standing.

An hour and a half went by. Then, rising to his feet, the kapalik addressed Nabokumar in Sanskrit, as before. 'Follow me,' he ordered.

At any other time, Nabokumar would certainly not have accompanied him. But now he complied, because hunger and thirst had made him desperate.

'As you say, sir,' he answered. 'But I am starving. Where could I find some food, by your leave?'

'The goddess has sent you to me,' answered the kapalik, in Sanskrit. 'Follow me; you will be satisfied.'

Nabokumar followed the kapalik. They trudged a long distance, the two of them, without speaking a word to each other. At last, they reached a thatched hut. Entering first, the kapalik allowed Nabokumar in, and by some mysterious means incomprehensible to the young man, ignited a piece of firewood. By the light of that flame, Nabokumar saw that the entire hut was built of keya leaves. Within the hut were some tiger skins, a pitcher of water and some fruit.

Having lit a fire, the kapalik told him: 'You may have all the fruit, and use a cupped leaf to drink from the pitcher. Recline on the tiger skins if you so desire. You may rest in peace, for there is no fear of tigers here. You will see me again after a while; until then, don't leave this hut.'

With these words, the kapalik departed. Nabokumar ate the fruits and drank the slightly brackish water, with immense satisfaction. Stretching out on a tiger skin, exhausted after the events of the day, he soon fell into a deep slumber.

On the Seashore

In you, no sign of spiritual influence can be seen;
Your aspect is sad, like Mrinalini, suffering from the cold.
Raghuvamsha

When he awakened at dawn, Nabokumar instinctively struggled to find a means of returning home. He thought it especially unwise to remain in the proximity of this kapalik. But how, at this juncture, was he to escape from this pathless forest? And how would he find his way back home? The kapalik surely knew the way: would he not offer directions, if requested? Since the kapalik, so far, had not displayed any threatening tendencies towards him, why should Nabokumar be afraid? On the other hand, the kapalik had forbidden him to leave the hut until they met again, and was likely to be angered if his injunctions were disobeyed. Having heard that kapaliks possessed the magic powers to accomplish the impossible, Nabokumar deemed it unwise to disobey this man. All things considered, he decided to remain in the hut for the time being.

But the day wore on, and the kapalik did not return. After a whole day of fasting, the lack of food this morning made Nabokumar acutely hungry. The previous night, he had already devoured all the fruit he found in the hut. Now, if he did not venture forth in search of fruits and vegetables, he would surely die of starvation. With just a few hours of daylight remaining, Nabokumar set out to gather some fruit.

He scoured the sand hills for fruit. Sampling the fruits on the few trees that grew in that sandy soil, he quelled his hunger pangs with a particular fruit that had the delicious flavour of almonds.

As the stretch of sand dunes was rather narrow, Nabokumar crossed the dunes in a very short time. He now found himself in a dense forest, devoid of sand. Anyone who has spent a short time roaming in an unfamiliar forest would know how easy it is to lose one's way in a pathless jungle. So it was with Nabokumar. Having walked a short distance, he could not remember the way back to the ashram. Hearing the deep sound of turbulent waters, he recognised it as the roar of the ocean. Soon after, he suddenly found himself out of the forest, facing the sea. His heart leapt with joy at the sight of this vast, blue expanse of water. He reclined on the sandy shore. Before him stretched the ocean, foaming, blue, limitless. On both sides, as far as the eye could see, was a line of froth, flung onshore by the breaking waves, like a garland of bunched white blossoms deposited on the golden sand, a hair ornament to adorn the earth's green tresses. Foaming waves broke the blue surface of the water in a thousand places. Only a storm violent enough to displace thousands of stars, swirling them against the azure backdrop of the sky, could match the sight of the waves churning in the ocean. At this moment, one segment of the blue water shone like molten gold in the gentle rays of the setting sun. Far away, a European merchant vessel breasted the waves, white sails outspread, winging its way like some gigantic bird.

Nabokumar had no idea how long he remained on the seashore, gazing at the beauty of the ocean. Then, the darkness of dusk descended upon the black waters. It now struck Nabokumar that he must locate the ashram. He rose to his feet with a sigh. Why he sighed, I cannot say, for there is no telling what happy memories awakened in his heart at that moment. Rising to his feet, he turned away from the sea. At once, he beheld an extraordinary apparition. At the edge of the wave-resonant ocean, on the sandy shore, in the blurred glow of twilight, stood an exquisite female figure! Outlined against her heavy tresses – her thick, unbraided locks, coiled like snakes, cascading down to her ankles – her body glowed like a jewel, a picture framed by its backdrop. Though partially concealed by the profusion of her hair, her countenance glowed like moonlight glimpsed through a gap in the clouds. Her large eyes were calm, tender and intense, yet bright as the gentle moonbeams that played upon the ocean's breast. Her shoulders were completely obscured from view by her cascading hair, but the unblemished beauty of her arms was partially visible. Her body was free of ornament. The magic of her beauty was indescribable. The enchanting effect of her complexion, resembling the gleam of the crescent moon, offset by the tangled webs of her dark hair, had to be viewed against the backdrop of that wave-resonant sea-shore, in the twilight glow, for its true impact to be felt.

Suddenly encountering this divine figure in the midst of such a wilderness, Nabokumar stood transfixed. Robbed of speech, he gazed at her in silence. She, too, fixed the unwavering, unblinking gaze of her enormous eyes on Nabokumar's face. But Nabokumar's eyes bore a startled expression, while the young woman showed no signs of surprise; instead, her gaze expressed acute anxiety.

There the two of them remained, on the vast ocean's desolate shore, gazing at each other in this way, for a very long time. After a prolonged silence, the young woman's voice was heard.

'Traveller, have you lost your way?' she asked, very softly.

Her voice struck the chords in Nabokumar's heart. The strings of our heart's extraordinary instrument sometimes grow too slack to be tuned to harmony, try as one might. But at a single sound, at the musical note in a woman's voice, the dissonance is instantly rectified. All the strings fall into tune. At such a moment, the journey of life seems to resemble a blissful stream of music. The sound of her voice fell upon Nabokumar's ears with just such an effect.

'Traveller, have you lost your way?' The sound of the words entered his ears. What they meant, what reply he should offer, he did not know. The sound seemed to spread everywhere, bringing a shiver of joy; it seemed to fill the breeze and murmur through the leaves on the trees, fading away to blend with the ocean's booming sound. The earth, girdled with the sea, was beautiful; beautiful, too, was the woman, and also the sound of her voice. The heart's instrument began to resonate with the rhythms of harmony.

'Come with me,' invited the maiden, when she received no reply to her question. With these words, she walked away, leaving no footprints. With invisible footsteps she moved, like a white cloud wafted on the slow spring breeze; like a clockwork toy, Nabokumar followed. At a certain place, where they had to skirt a small wood, the beautiful maiden disappeared behind a clump of trees. Having trudged around the forested area, Nabokumar found himself standing before a hut.

With the Kapalik

Alas, why are you in chains? I shall take you hence, forthwith!
Ratnabali

Entering the hut, Nabokumar closed the door and sank to the floor, clasping his head in his hands. He did not raise his head for a long time.

'Is she a goddess, a human being, or merely an illusion conjured up by the kapalik?' Frozen, immobile, he turned this question over and over in his mind, uncomprehending.

Preoccupied as he was, Nabokumar failed to notice something else. Inside the hut, even before his arrival, there was already a burning torch. The improbability of it struck him only afterwards, late at night, when he remembered that his evening ablutions had not been performed, his reverie disrupted by the task of fetching water. In the hut, he found not only a lighted torch, but also some rice and other provisions. He was not surprised, taking it for another sign of the kapalik's diligence. In this place, nothing seemed surprising anymore. Having completed his evening chores, Nabokumar dined on rice, cooked in an earthen vessel that he found in the hut.

The next morning, as soon as he left his bed made of animal skin, he headed for the seashore. Thanks to the previous day's explorations, he did not have much trouble finding his way. Once there, morning ablutions over, he waited. Who was he waiting for? How intensely Nabokumar longed for last evening's enchantress to reappear at this spot, I cannot say for certain; but he was unable to leave the place. The day advanced, but no one appeared. Nabokumar began to roam about restlessly. He searched in vain, unable to detect the faintest trace of human habitation. He came back to the same spot as before. The sun set and it grew dark. Despondently, Nabokumar retraced his steps to the hut. Returning from the seashore at dusk, he found the kapalik seated silently on the floor of the hut. The kapalik did not return Nabokumar's greetings.

'Why was I denied access to the master until now?' asked Nabokumar.

'I was occupied with my own religious rituals.'

Nabokumar then expressed his desire to return to his homeland. 'I don't know the way,' he explained. 'Nor have I any provisions for the journey. I have been surviving on the hope that a meeting with the master will indicate my next course of action.'

'Come with me,' was all the kapalik said. He rose to his feet with an indifferent air. Nabokumar followed him, hoping to find some proper means of making his way back home.

The glow of twilight had not yet faded. The kapalik strode on ahead, with Nabokumar following behind. Suddenly, Nabokumar felt a tender touch on his back. Turning, he froze at the sight that met his eyes. It was the same goddess of the wilderness, she of the dense, ankle-length tresses! As before, she was silent and utterly still. From where had this vision suddenly appeared? The maiden had placed a finger on her lips; Nabokumar realised she was warning him against blurting out anything. Not that any warning was required. What could Nabokumar have said? Wonderstruck, he remained rooted to the spot. The kapalik walked on ahead, unaware. Once he was out of earshot, the maiden spoke, in a low, gentle voice.

'Where are you going?' Nabokumar heard her murmur. 'Stop! Turn back! Run away!'

The words were barely out of her mouth before she moved away, without waiting for a reply. For a while, Nabokumar remained rooted to the spot, stupefied. He was anxious to turn back, but could not determine the direction in which the maiden had vanished.

'Who has cast this magic spell?' he began to wonder. 'Or have I become disoriented? The words I heard are frightening, indeed, but what is the cause for fear? Tantriks are capable of anything. Should I run away, then? But why should I escape? If I could survive yesterday's events, I shall survive today, as well. The kapalik is a man, and so am I.'

As he pondered these things, Nabokumar saw the kapalik returning in search of him.

'Why do you tarry?' demanded the kapalik.

At this second call, Nabokumar followed the kapalik without a word.

Having trudged a short distance, they came upon a mud-walled hut. It could even be called a small house, but that does not concern us. Immediately behind was the sandy shore of the sea. Skirting the house, the kapalik led Nabokumar towards that shore. Suddenly, with the speed of an arrow, the maiden darted past the young man.

'Escape, even now!' she whispered into his ear in passing. 'Don't you know a tantrik's prayers are never complete without an offering of human flesh?'

Nabokumar's forehead broke out in sweat. Unfortunately, the maiden's words had reached the ears of the kapalik.

'Kapalkundala!' he roared.

His voice fell upon Nabokumar's ears like the rumble of thunder in the clouds. But Kapalkundala offered no reply.

The kapalik began to drag Nabokumar by the hand. At his deadly touch, the blood began to pound in Nabokumar's veins, and he recovered the courage he had lost.

'Release my hand,' he demanded. The kapalik made no reply.

'Where are you taking me?' Nabokumar persisted.

'To the place for prayer,' answered the kapalik.

'Why?'

'To sacrifice you.'

Swiftly, Nabokumar tried to wrench his hand away from his grasp. The force of his action should not only have freed his hand, but also flung an ordinary mortal to the ground. But the kapalik did not budge an inch; Nabokumar's wrist remained fast within his grip. The young man's bones and tendons seemed to crumble under the pressure. Nabokumar realised that words would not save him. Subterfuge was the need of the hour.

'Very well, we'll see what happens,' he decided, allowing the kapalik to drag him along.

Once they reached the appointed spot in the middle of the sandy stretch, Nabokumar saw a huge log fire burning there, as before. Arranged around the fire were the trappings of a tantrik ritual, including liquor-filled human skulls, but no corpse. He gathered that he was meant to serve as the corpse.

Some dry, sinewy vines had already been placed there. The kapalik proceeded to bind Nabokumar's limbs tightly with them. Nabokumar tried to resist with all his might, but to no effect. Even at this advanced age, the kapalik had the strength of a mad elephant, he realised.

'You fool!' exclaimed the kapalik, observing Nabokumar's attempts to assert his strength. 'Why do you try to show your might? Today, your life has become worthwhile. To surrender your flesh to the worship of the goddess – what better fortune could a man like you desire?'

Having bound Nabokumar securely, the kapalik flung him down on the sand. He then busied himself with prayers and rituals, in preparation for the human sacrifice. Meanwhile, Nabokumar struggled to free himself; but the dry vines were too tough for him, the bonds too strong. Death was near at hand! Nabokumar now turned his mind to prayer. He remembered, in a flash, his birthplace, his comfortable home, his long-departed parents. He shed a few teardrops, instantly absorbed by the sand. Preliminary rituals over, the kapalik rose to his feet, looking for the scimitar with which the sacrifice was to be performed. But the scimitar was not where he had placed it. How extraordinary! The kapalik was rather surprised. He distinctly remembered having put the scimitar in its proper place that afternoon, and he had not removed it since. Where could it have gone? The kapalik searched here and there, but the scimitar was nowhere to be found. Then, turning towards the aforementioned cottage, he shouted for Kapalkundala, but his repeated calls went unanswered. The kapalik's eyes grew fiery red, his eyebrows twisted in a frown. He strode off in the direction of his own abode. Nabokumar took this opportunity to try once more to break free of the wild vines that bound him; but even these attempts were futile. Then he heard gentle footsteps on the sand. This was not the kapalik's tread.

Turning around, Nabokumar beheld the same enchantress as before – Kapalkundala! In her hand, swaying to and fro, was the scimitar.

'Shh! Don't say a word!' she cautioned him. 'I have the scimitar – I stole it!'

With these words, wielding the scimitar, she began to quickly sever the bonds that tied Nabokumar. In an instant, he was free.

'Run away!' she urged. 'Follow me, I'll show you the way.'

Swift as an arrow, she sped on ahead, leading the way. Nabokumar raced after her.

The Hunt

And the great lord of Luna
Fell at that deadly stroke;
As falls on mount Alvemus
A thunder-smitten oak.
Lays of Ancient Rome

Meanwhile, the kapalik, having scoured the interior of his hut without finding either the scimitar or Kapalkundala, returned to the sand dunes in a suspicious frame of mind. He was astounded to discover that Nabokumar had vanished. Soon, he noticed the severed fragments of the vines that had bound the young man. Understanding the truth of the matter, the kapalik rushed away in search of Nabokumar. But in the desolate wilderness, it was hard to determine which way the fugitives may have gone. Unable to see anyone in the dark, he wandered here and there for a while, listening for voices. But he could hear no voices, either. To scrutinise his surroundings, he now climbed to the top of a high sand dune. He ascended the slope on one side, unaware that the flow of water had eroded the base of the sand dune on the opposite side. As soon as he reached the top, the kapalik's body weight caused the dune's crest to collapse with a resounding crash. Like a bull dislodged from a mountain peak, the kapalik, too, fell with the descending mass of sand.

Refuge

And that very night –
Shall Romeo bear thee to Mantua.
Romeo and Juliet

Breathlessly they raced into the forest, the two of them, in the darkness of that moonless night. Unfamiliar with the forest tracks, Nabokumar had no choice but to follow the path taken by his young female companion, keeping her in sight. 'Fate had this, too, in store for me!' he thought to himself. Nabokumar did not know that Bengalis are slaves of circumstance, not masters of their situation. Else, he would not have felt so aggrieved.

Gradually, they slackened their pace. In the darkness, nothing could be seen, but for the white crest of an occasional sand dune, outlined indistinctly in the starlight, or the shape of a tree trunk, adorned with its garland of foliage.

Kapalkundala led her fellow-traveller into a desolate garden. The night was far advanced. Before them, in the darkness, a tall temple dome loomed above the trees of the forest. Near it, they could also see a house made of brick, encircled by a wall. Approaching the wall, Kapalkundala knocked on the gate.

'Who is that?' called a male voice from within, after repeated knocking. 'Is it Kapalkundala?'

'Open the door!' cried Kapalkundala.

The door was opened by the man who had answered from within. About fifty years of age, he was the officiating priest who attended upon the deity of the temple. Drawing down his hairless head, Kapalkundala brought her lips close to his ear and briefly explained her companion's predicament. For a long while, the priest pondered, resting his head in his hands.

'This is a terrible affair,' he presently declared. 'Once he makes up his mind, the kapalik is capable of anything. Anyway, by the grace of Ma, our presiding deity, no harm will come to you. Where is the person in question?'

Kapalkundala called out to Nabokumar, who had remained out of sight. Upon her invitation, he entered the house.

'Hide here, today,' advised the priest. 'Tomorrow, at dawn, I shall take you to the road that leads to Medinipur.'

In the course of conversation, it dawned on the priest that Nabokumar was starving. He busied himself preparing a meal for the young man, but Nabokumar had no appetite, and begged only for a place to rest. The priest arranged a bed for him in his own kitchen. When Nabokumar had retired for the night, Kapalkundala prepared to return to the seashore.

'Please don't leave!' begged the priest, looking at her with affection. 'Wait a little. I have a humble request.'

'What is it?'

'Ever since I set my eyes on you, I have addressed you as "Ma",' pleaded the priest. 'I touch the deity's feet and swear that I adore you as my mother, and more. You will not spurn my request, will you?'

'I will not.'

'I beseech you not to return to that place.'

'Why not?'

'You cannot save yourself if you do.'

'Indeed, I know that's true.'

'Then why ask for reasons?'

'Where else can I go?'

'Go with this traveller to another part of the country.'

Kapalkundala remained silent.

'What are you thinking, Ma?' asked the priest.

'When your disciple had come here earlier, you had said that it was inappropriate for a young woman to accompany a young man. Now, why do you ask me to do the same thing?'

'I had not feared for your life at that time. What's more important, there was no proper solution available at that time, but such a solution may be possible now. Come, let's seek the deity's consent.'

Lamp in hand, the priest went to the door of the temple and unlocked it. Kapalkundala joined him. Inside the temple was the awesome image of goddess Kali in human form. They offered their devotion, the two of them, at the deity's feet. The priest performed some preliminary rituals before chanting a prayer over an intact triad of belpata, wood-apple leaves, which he placed at the idol's feet. He gazed at the leaves for a while.

'Look, Ma, the devi has accepted our offering,' he pointed out to Kapalkundala. 'The leaves didn't fall off, which means the wish I made while making the offering is bound to come true. You may proceed with this traveller with no misgivings. But I know the ways of worldly men. If you accompany him as an appendage, he will find the company of an unknown young woman a social embarrassment. People will also treat you with contempt. You tell me this man is a Brahmin; I see he wears a sacred thread. It would be best for everyone concerned if he were to marry you. Otherwise, even I cannot bring myself to say that you should accompany him.'

'M-a-r-r-y!' Kapalkundala pronounced the word very slowly. 'I hear all of you speak of marriage, but I don't know exactly what it means. What does marriage require of me?'

'Marriage is a woman's only stepping stone to dharma, the observance of her sacred duty,' explained the priest, with a faint smile. 'That is why a wife is called a sahadharmini, a man's partner in his pursuit of dharma. Even Jaganmata, divine mother of the world, is married to Shiva.'

The priest thought he had explained everything. Kapalkundala thought she had understood everything.

'So let it be,' she assented. 'But I don't feel like abandoning my foster father. After all, he has taken care of me, all this time.'

'Don't you know why he has taken such care of you?'

The priest tried to explain to Kapalkundala, in a roundabout way, the role of a woman in tantrik prayer rituals. Kapalkundala did not understand anything of this, but she felt very frightened.

'Very well, let the marriage take place, then,' she faltered.

They emerged from the temple. Leaving Kapalkundala in one of the rooms, the priest approached the sleeping Nabokumar.

'Are you asleep, sir?' he enquired.

'No, sir,' answered Nabokumar. Unable to sleep, he was worrying about his own predicament.

'Sir, I have come to request an introduction,' the priest explained. 'Are you a Brahmin?'

'Yes, sir.'

'Of what category?'

'Radhi.'

'We, too, are Radhi Brahmins. Don't take us for Utkal Brahmins. By birth, I am head-priest of my clan, but at this moment, I have taken refuge at the deity's feet. What is sir's name?'

'Nabokumar Sharma.'

'Place of residence?'

'Saptagram.'

'Which village do you come from?'

'Bandyaghoti.'

'How many families do you have?'

'Just one.' Nabokumar did not disclose the entire truth. Actually, he did not have even one family. He had married Padmavati, daughter of Ramgobinda Ghoshal. After the wedding, Padmavati had remained in her paternal home for some time, visiting her in-laws occasionally. When she was thirteen, her father had taken his family on a pilgrimage to the shrine of Purushottam. At this time, the Pathans, expelled from Bengal by Emperor Akbar, had collectively settled in Orissa. Emperor Akbar was now systematically engaged in the task of curbing them. When Ramgobinda Ghoshal set out on his journey back from Orissa, fighting had broken out between the Mughals and the Pathans. On the way, he fell into the hands of the Pathan army. The Pathans, at that time, did not discriminate between the respectable and the disreputable; they tried to threaten the innocent traveller, in the hope of extorting money. Somewhat aggressive by nature, Ramgobinda began to shower abuses upon them. As a result, he and his family were taken captive. Ultimately, they saved themselves by converting to Islam, surrendering their faith.

Ramgobinda Ghoshal returned alive, along with his family; but as a Muslim, he was now ostracised by his own community. Under these circumstances, Nabokumar's father, who was alive at the time, had no choice but to disown his daughter-in-law and also her father, for having lost their caste purity. Nabokumar did not see his wife again.

Cast out by his family and his community, Ramgobinda Ghoshal could not remain in his hometown for long. For this reason, and also from an ambitious desire to attain a high position in the royal household, he moved with his family to the capital city, and settled in the royal palace there. Having converted to Islam, he and his family had adopted Muslim names. Once they had moved into the royal palace, Nabokumar had no way of finding out what became of the father and his daughter; and indeed, up to this time, he had no information about them. He was too detached to marry again. That is why I say Nabokumar had no family at all.

The temple attendant was unaware of these facts. 'Why should a kulin Brahmin object to having two families?' he thought.

Outwardly, he said: 'I had come to make a request. This young woman who saved your life has wasted her life in the service of another. The holy man who has given her refuge is a person to be dreaded. If she returns to him, she will meet the same fate that was designed for you. Can't you think of a way out for her?'

Nabokumar sat up. 'That's what I had feared,' he confessed. 'You know the whole story: please suggest a solution. I am willing to lay down my life if required, by way of reciprocating her goodwill. I am thinking of going back to that murderer, to surrender myself to him. That should save her life.'

'You are insane!' laughed the official. 'What good would that do? You would lose your life, but that would not reduce the holy man's ire against this girl. There is only one solution to the problem.'

'What is it?'

'She must run away with you. But that is very difficult to accomplish. If she remains here with me, she will be captured within a couple of days. The holy man visits this temple regularly. It seems apparent to me that fate doesn't augur well for Kapalkundala.'

'Why would it be so difficult for her to escape with me?' demanded Nabokumar, eagerly.

'You know nothing about her – her parentage, her caste. Would you accept her as your companion? Even if you did, would you offer her a place in your home? And if you don't let her stay with you, where will this orphan go?'

'There's nothing I cannot do for the person who saved my life,' answered Nabokumar, after pausing briefly to consider. 'She will live with me as a member of my family.'

'Very well. But when your relatives want to know whose wife she is, what answer will you offer?'

Nabokumar paused again to consider. 'Please explain her parentage to me,' he requested. 'That is how I shall introduce her to everyone.'

'Fine,' replied the priest. 'But how will a young man and a young woman travel unchaperoned across the border from one region to another? What will people say? How will you explain this to your relatives? And having adopted this girl as my Ma, how can I send her off to some faraway place in the company of an unknown young man?'

The matchmaker was quite skilled at his job!

'You could accompany us,' Nabokumar suggested.

'Accompany you? Who would offer daily prayers to Goddess Bhavani then?'

'Can you think of no solution, then?' demanded Nabokumar, aggrieved.

'There can be only one solution. It depends on your magnanimity.'

'What is it? Is there anything I would refuse? Please tell me what the solution might be!'

'Then listen. She is the daughter of a Brahmin. I know the entire story of her life. In her childhood, she was abducted by a band of dreaded Christian brigands, who abandoned her on this seashore after their carriage broke down. Later, you can ask her for a detailed account of this story. The kapalik found her, and brought her up with the intention of using her to fulfil the requirements of his religious practice. In the near future, he would have satisfied his own needs. She is still chaste, pure of nature. Marry her and take her home with you. Nobody can raise any objections then. I shall conduct the wedding rites according to the scriptures.'

Nabokumar rose to his feet and began to pace swiftly up and down. He offered no reply.

'Please go back to sleep,' advised the temple attendant after a while. 'I shall wake you at dawn. You may travel alone if you wish. I shall show you the road to Medinipur.'

With these words, he took his leave. 'Have I forgotten the art of matchmaking which I learnt in the land of Radh?' he wondered to himself, as he departed.

In the Temple

Kanwa: Weep no more. Be calm. Walk this way, watching your step.
Shakuntala

At dawn, the priest approached Nabokumar, to find that the young man had not slept at all.

'What is to be our course of action?' the priest inquired.

'From today, Kapalkundala shall be my wife,' declared Nabokumar. 'For her sake, I could even renounce the world. Who will give away the bride?'

The expert matchmaker's countenance glowed with joy. 'At last, by the grace of goddess Jagadamba, my little Kapalini seems to have found a way out of her predicament!' he thought to himself. Outwardly, he said, 'I shall give away the bride.'

The priest returned to his bedroom, where a few worn and faded palm-leaf parchments had been stored inside a khungi, a small cane casket. Inscribed on the palm leaves was the almanac, which charted auspicious days, astronomical calculations, etc. Having closely scrutinised the almanac, he emerged from his room and announced:

'Today is not a date earmarked for weddings, but there are no obstacles indicated for a marriage ceremony on this day. At dusk, I shall perform the kanyadaan ritual to give away the bride. A daylong fast is all you need observe. Ensure that all other family rituals are performed after you return to your own home. There is a place where I can conceal the two of you for a day. If the kapalik comes here today, he will not find you. Once married, you can leave for home at daybreak tomorrow, accompanied by your wife.'

Nabokumar agreed to this proposal. The ceremony was performed, following the prescribed rules as closely as the present circumstances permitted. At dusk, Nabokumar was married to the hermit woman, the kapalik's foster daughter.

There was no sign of the kapalik. Early next morning, the three of them prepared to set out on their journey. The priest would accompany them up to the road to Medinipur.

When it was time to leave, Kapalkundala went to pay her last respects to the image of Kali. In deep devotion, she bowed in obeisance; then, taking an intact belpata triad from the flower basket, she placed it at the deity's feet, and fixed her gaze upon it. The belpata fell off.

Kapalkundala was deeply religious. She was terrified to see the triple leaf fall away from the feet of the idol. She informed the priest, who was also perturbed.

'There is nothing to be done, now,' he told her. 'Your husband is now your sole object of devotion. If he heads for the cremation ground, even there you must follow him. So, you must now proceed quietly on your journey.'

The three of them trudged on in silence. The day was far advanced when they arrived at the road to Medinipur. The priest took his leave of them. Kapalkundala burst into tears.

She was parting with the person dearest to her in the whole world.

The priest also began to weep. Then, wiping away his tears, he whispered to Kapalkundala: 'Ma! You know that, by the grace of the goddess, I do not lack for means. The goddess receives prayer offerings from everyone in Hijli, old or young. Use what I have knotted into the end of your sari – give it to your husband, and ask him to hire a palanquin for you. Think of me as your son!'

Weeping, he departed. Also in tears, Kapalkundala proceeded on her journey.

Part 2

On the Highway

There – now lean on me:
Place your foot here –
Manfred

When they arrived at Medinipur, Nabokumar arranged a palanquin for Kapalkundala, using the money donated by the priest to hire a maid, a bodyguard and palanquin bearers. Due to paucity of funds, he himself proceeded on foot. Nabokumar was exhausted after the strain of the previous day. After their noontime meal, the palanquin bearers outstripped him, leaving him far behind. As evening approached, the daylight waned. The sky was overcast with light winter clouds. Then, the twilight faded, too, and darkness enveloped the earth. It began to drizzle. Nabokumar now grew anxious to catch up with Kapalkundala. He was certain that he would find her at the first serai, or wayside inn, but there was no serai in sight at present. The hour was late. Nabokumar strode on swiftly. Suddenly, he trod on something hard; it broke under his weight with a loud, cracking sound. Nabokumar paused, then walked on. The same thing happened again. He bent to pick up the object he had stepped on. It looked like a broken plank of wood.

Even on a cloudy night, it is not usually dark enough, out in the open, for a solid shape to remain entirely invisible. Before him lay a giant object, which Nabokumar realised was a broken palanquin. At once, he was filled with apprehensions of some danger having befallen Kapalkundala. As he advanced towards the palanquin, his foot again touched something. This time, the substance felt different, like the touch of tender human flesh. Kneeling to stroke the form that lay on the ground, he found that it was indeed a human body. It was extremely cold to the touch; his fingers felt something wet. He could not find the pulse: the person was dead. But when he listened carefully, the sound of breathing could be heard. If breath remained, why was there no pulse? Was this person ill? Placing his hand close to the nostrils, he could feel no breath. Then why that sound? Perhaps there was also a living person present on the scene.

'Is there a living person here?' he asked.

'There is,' came the reply, in a low voice.

'Who are you?'

'Who are *you*?' demanded the voice, in return.

The voice sounded like a woman's.

'Kapalkundala, is that you?' asked Nabokumar, in great agitation.

'Who Kapalkundala is, I don't know,' replied the woman. 'I am a traveller, with no kundals or earrings to my name at present, thanks to the bandits who have robbed me.'

Her wit lightened Nabokumar's mood somewhat. 'What's the matter?' he asked.

'The bandits have smashed my palanquin,' replied the woman. 'They have killed one of the bearers, and the others have run away. Having robbed me of all the jewels I was wearing, the bandits have tied me up and left me here inside the palanquin.'

Groping in the dark, Nabokumar found that there was indeed a woman lying inside the palanquin, trussed up by some garments. Swiftly, he untied her bonds.

'Can you get up?' he asked.

'They struck me with a stick,' the woman replied. 'My leg hurts. But with a bit of help, I think I can stand up.'

Nabokumar extended his hand, and with his support, the woman rose to her feet.

'Can you walk?' asked Nabokumar.

'Did you see any other traveller following you?' the woman enquired, without answering his question.

'No.'

'How far is it to the chati, the wayside resting-place?' she wanted to know.

'I couldn't say exactly, but I suppose it's not far away.'

'It's no use sitting alone here, out in the open,' decided the woman. 'I should go with you up to the chati. I can probably hobble along with some support.'

'It's foolish to harbour scruples in times of crisis,' declared Nabokumar. 'You can lean on my shoulder.'

The woman was not foolish enough to hesitate; she began to walk, leaning on his shoulder for support.

The chati was indeed not far away. Those days, bandits were not afraid to commit robberies even near a chati. Within a short time, Nabokumar arrived at the resting place, along with his companion.

There, he found Kapalkundala. Her attendants had hired a room for her. Nabokumar hired an adjoining room for his fellow-traveller, and ensconced her there. At his request, the landlady's daughter brought in a lighted oil lamp. Bathed in the stream of lamplight, his companion's body struck Nabokumar as extraordinarily beautiful. Her voluptuous beauty resembled the surging waves of a river in the monsoon flood.

The Wayside Inn

Who is this woman, so restless by nature?
Uddhavduta

If this woman's beauty had been flawless, I would have said: 'O male reader! She is as beautiful as your own wife. And O my beautiful female reader! She is as lovely as your own image in the mirror.' Her appearance would need no further description.

Unfortunately, she was not beautiful in every respect; hence I cannot adopt that course.

She was not a flawless beauty: firstly, she was slightly above medium height; secondly, her lips were rather thin; and thirdly, she was not really fair of complexion.

She was rather tall, indeed, but her limbs and bosom were full and well-rounded. Like trees and vines in the rainy season, her body rippled with its own voluptuousness, the fullness lending grace even to her tall figure. A truly fair complexion resembles either the light of the full moon, or the rosy light of dawn. I do not describe this woman as truly fair because her complexion resembled neither; but her colouring was no less attractive. She was dusky, but hers was not the dark complexion evoked by the names of 'Shyama Ma', the goddess Kali, or 'Shyam Sundar', the lord Krishna. Her skin had the deep hue of molten gold. If the light of the full moon or the rays of the golden sun are similes for the fair-complexioned, then the glory of vernal foliage may be an apt analogy for the complexion of this dusky woman. Many of my esteemed readers may celebrate the complexion of fair-skinned women, but if anyone comes under the spell of such a dark-complexioned woman, I would not call him colour-blind. If anyone should quarrel with this view, let him imagine this woman, her locks clustered about her dark, glowing forehead like bees hovering about the petals of a newly blossomed flower; her eyebrows, arching up to her hairline beneath her crescent-shaped brow; her cheeks, bright as flowers in full bloom, and her small, rosy mouth. Visualising her thus, he is bound to find this unknown woman beautiful, on the whole. Her eyes were not large, but they were extremely bright, and framed by lovely, curling lashes. Their gaze was calm, yet penetrating. Her glance would instantly make you feel that she had the power to look into the interior of your heart. The expression of those penetrating eyes would change from moment to moment, now melting with tender affection, now full of sweet languor, as if the god of love himself lay dreaming there. At times, her eyes would be dilated with desire, intoxicated with romance; and at other times, a heartless sidelong glance would dart from the corners of her eyes, like a flash of lightning in the clouds. Two ineffable elements irradiated her countenance: the stamp of intelligence, and her self-esteem. From her posture, the arch of her swan neck, it was clear that she was a queen among women.

This beautiful woman was twenty-seven years old, in the full flush of youth, like a river in flood during the month of Bhadra. Her sensuous beauty brimmed over, like a river surging against its banks in the rains. Even more than her complexion, her eyes, and all her individual features, this floodtide of voluptuousness, rendered her enchanting. Youthful vitality made her body restless, as a river in autumn ripples even without a breeze; from moment to moment, this restless energy revealed some new facet of her loveliness. Nabokumar gazed, transfixed, at this ever-changing display of charm.

'What are you staring at? My beauty?' enquired the beautiful woman, observing his unblinking stare.

Nabokumar was a bhadralok, a gentleman; embarrassed, he lowered his gaze.

Seeing that he was speechless, the unknown woman smiled. 'Have you never seen a woman before?' she persisted, 'or do you find me so very beautiful?'

Because she smiled, what would normally have seemed a reprimand sounded merely like a sarcastic remark. Nabokumar realised that she was extremely articulate. Why should he not engage in repartee with such a loquacious woman?

'I have indeed seen other women,' he replied. 'But I have not seen anyone so lovely.'

'Not even one?' she enquired, with pride.

In his mind's eye, Nabokumar saw a vision of Kapalkundala. 'I wouldn't quite say that,' he answered, with equal arrogance.

'That's not so bad, then. Is she your wife, the other one?'

'Why? Why should you imagine her to be my wife?'

'Bengalis find their own wives most beautiful.'

'I am a Bengali. You sound like a Bengali, too. Where are you from?'

'Yours truly is not fortunate enough to be a Bengali,' replied the young woman, glancing at her own attire. 'I am a Muslim from the western region.'

Inspecting her appearance, Nabokumar realised that her garb was indeed that of a Muslim woman from the west. But she spoke Bengali exactly as if it were her mother tongue.

'Sir, you have taken my measure in repartee,' she continued, after a pause. 'Now please gratify me by disclosing your identity. Where is the home of which that woman of unparalleled beauty is the mistress?'

'I live in Saptagram,' answered Nabokumar.

The woman – this stranger from elsewhere – did not reply. Suddenly, she bent over the lamp and busied herself trying to turn up its flame.

'My name is Moti,' she informed him after a while, without raising her head. 'May I not know yours?'

'Nabokumar Sharma.'

The lamp went out.

A View of Female Beauty

…O goddess, as divine enchantress let yourself appear!
By your leave, with ornaments diverse,
Your beauteous form I shall adorn!
Meghnadbadh

44

Nabokumar ordered the landlord to fetch another lamp. Before the lamp arrived, he heard a sigh. Soon after, a Muslim in attendant's livery entered the room.

'What's this!' exclaimed the female stranger. 'Why did you take so long, all of you? Where are the others?'

'The bearers were drunk!' replied the attendant. 'While we struggled to herd them together, your palanquin left us far behind. Afterwards, discovering the smashed palanquin, and no sign of you anywhere, we almost fainted with shock. Some of them are still at that spot; others have scattered here and there in search of you. I came here looking for you.'

'Get them to this place!' ordered Moti.

Saluting her, the attendant departed. The woman from elsewhere remained lost in thought for a while, resting her cheek on her hand.

Nabokumar prepared to leave. Like a sleepwalker, Moti rose to her feet.

'Where will you stay?' she asked, resuming her earlier tone.

'In the very next room.'

'I saw a palanquin near that room. Do you have a companion?'

'My wife accompanies me.'

'Is she the one, the woman of unparalleled beauty?' asked Moti, finding another opportunity for banter.

'If you see her, you will know.'

'Would it be possible to see her?'

'What's the harm?' replied Nabokumar, after some thought.

'Do me a favour, then. I am very curious to see this woman, this matchless beauty. I want to speak of her when I get to Agra. But not now. Please leave me now. I shall send word to you after some time.'

Nabokumar left. Soon after, a large contingent arrived there, including attendants, maidservants, and bearers carrying chests and other items of luggage. With them came a palanquin, bearing a maidservant. Then Nabokumar received a message: 'Bibi, her ladyship, is thinking of you.'

Nabokumar returned to Motibibi. Once again, he found her transformed. She had shed her earlier garb, and was now attired in embroidered garments, embellished with gold and pearls; her person, previously bare of ornament, was now bedecked with jewellery. Gold, diamonds and precious stones flashed from every part of her body, from her tresses and braided hair-knot to her forehead, temples, ears, throat, bosom, and both her arms. Nabokumar's eyes were dazzled. Like a garland of stars adorning the sky, the profusion of jewellery seemed appropriate for her voluptuous body, enhancing her charm.

'Come, Sir, let's get acquainted with your wife,' she invited Nabokumar.

'There was no need for you to adorn yourself with jewels for that purpose,' Nabokumar informed her. 'My wife has no ornaments at all.'

'Perhaps I have worn my jewellery to show it off. If a woman possesses ornaments, she can't resist displaying them. Let's go.'

Nabokumar escorted Motibibi from the room. Accompanying them was Peshaman, the maidservant who had arrived in the palanquin.

They found Kapalkundala alone, on the damp, earthen floor of the room that served as the shop. The room was faintly lit by a single lamp. Her form was framed by the dark backdrop of her heavy, unbound tresses. Glancing at her for the first time, Motibibi showed faint signs of amusement, a slight smile playing at the corners of her mouth and the edges of her eyes. She raised the lamp to take a closer look at Kapalkundala. All her amusement evaporated, and her expression grew grave. She gazed, unblinking. Both were silent – Moti spellbound, Kapalkundala slightly surprised.

After a while, Moti began to take off her jewellery. One by one, she removed her ornaments, and adorned Kapalkundala with them. Kapalkundala said nothing.

'What are you doing?' Nabokumar expostulated.

Moti offered no reply.

'You were indeed right,' she remarked to Nabokumar, when she had parted with all her ornaments. 'Such a flower does not blossom even in the garden of a king. It is my regret that I could not display this profusion of beauty at the capital city. These ornaments are befitting only for her figure – that's why I have bedecked her with them. I hope that you, too, will sometimes adorn her with these jewels, and remember me – this woman from an alien land, so skilled at repartee.'

'Impossible!' cried Nabokumar, thunderstruck. 'These jewels are priceless! Why should I accept them?'

'By the grace of God, I have more. I shall not be bereft of ornaments. If it gives me happiness to adorn her with these jewels, why should you object?'

With these words, Motibibi departed, along with her maid.

'Bibijaan! Who is this man?' demanded Peshaman as soon as they were alone.

'Mera shauhar,' replied the young Muslim lady. 'He is my husband!'

The Palanquin Ride

...Swiftly, I discard
My bangles, necklace, hair-ornament, choker
Earrings, anklets, girdle
Megnadbadh

Let me tell you the fate of those ornaments. Motibibi sent a silver-enamelled ivory casket for storing the jewellery. The robbers had taken only a few of her ornaments, unable to grab anything beyond what they found close at hand.

Leaving a few of the ornaments on Kapalkundala's person, Nabokumar transferred the rest to the casket. The next morning, Motibibi left for Burdhwan, and Nabokumar for Saptragram, accompanied by his wife. Nabokumar helped Kapalkundala into the palanquin, and handed her the casket of jewels. The bearers soon outstripped Nabokumar and proceeded on their way. Kapalkundala opened the palanquin door to observe the scene around her. Seeing her, a beggar began to walk alongside the palanquin, asking for alms.

'But I have nothing,' Kapalkundala protested. 'What can I offer you?'

'How can you say that, Ma!' cried the beggar, pointing at the few ornaments she wore. 'Bedecked with diamonds and pearls, you say you have nothing to give!'

'If I gave you these ornaments, would you be satisfied?' asked Kapalkundala.

The beggar was surprised. His greed knew no bounds. 'I would be satisfied, indeed!' he instantly replied.

Artlessly, Kapalkundala handed him the jewellery, casket and all. She even gave away the ornaments on her person.

For a moment, the beggar was overwhelmed. The attendants remained unaware of what had taken place. The beggar's hesitation lasted but an instant. Then, glancing quickly all about him, he made off with the jewellery at top speed.

'Why did the beggar run away?' wondered Kapalkundala to herself.

Back Home

These words, though sayable before her female
   companions,
I'd whisper only in her ear, just for the pleasure of her
   touch
Meghdoot

Accompanied by Kapalkundala, Nabokumar returned to his
own place of domicile. Fatherless, he lived with his widowed
mother and his two sisters. The elder of the two was a widow;
the reader will not have the opportunity of making her acquain-
tance. Though married, the second sister, Shyamasundari, was
virtually a widow, because her husband was a kulin Brahmin.
She will make a few brief appearances in the story.

When Nabokumar returned home under altered circumstances, married to a hermit woman of unknown extraction,
there is no saying whether his relatives would have approved.
But as it turned out, he did not have to suffer much on this
account. Everyone had given up hope of his ever coming back,
for upon their return, Nabokumar's fellow-travellers had
spread rumours about his having been killed by a tiger. The
esteemed reader may think that these truth-sayers had reported
what they believed to be a fact; but this would be an underesti-
mation of their imaginative powers. Many of the travellers who
had returned, swore that they had actually seen Nabokumar fall
into the tiger's clutches. They argued about the dimensions of
the tiger, some estimating its length at about twelve feet, while
others insisted that it was almost twenty-one feet long.

'Anyway, I had a narrow escape!' declared the old traveller
we have encountered earlier. 'The tiger chased me first, but
I eluded him. Nabokumar was not as brave: he didn't manage
to get away.'

When these rumours reached the ears of Nabokumar's mother and sisters, the sound of wailing that arose within the house did not subside for several days. The news of her only son's demise had brought his mother to the brink of death. In this situation, when Nabokumar returned home accompanied by a wife, no one thought to enquire about his spouse's caste or parentage. They were blind with joy, all of them. Nabokumar's mother cordially performed the boron ritual to welcome the bride into the house.

Nabokumar was overjoyed to find Kapalkundala so warmly accepted as a member of the household. Fearing that she might be rejected by his family, he had expressed neither tenderness nor desire towards Kapalkundala even after she became his wife. Yet, it was her image that filled his heart. It was this apprehension that had held him back from instantly agreeing to the proposed marriage with Kapalkundala. Indeed, it was this apprehension that had deterred him from expressing his love for her even once, from the time they were married, until they reached his home. He had not allowed the slightest wave to rock the ocean of his love, though it was full to flooding. But now, his anxieties were dispelled. Like the wild torrent that gushes forth when a rock obstructing the water's flow is shattered, the sea of love in Nabokumar's heart surged and spilled over.

This love did not always express itself in words. It revealed itself in the expression in Nabokumar's eyes whenever he looked at Kapalkundala, for he would gaze at her transfixed, his eyes brimming with tears; in the way he sought her out on some imaginary pretext, even when there was no need; in his attempts to bring Kapalkundala's name into the conversation, even when it was out of context; in his striving, day and night, to ensure Kapalkundala's happiness and comfort; in the way he ceaselessly paced up and down, lost in thought. Even his personality began to change. In place of restlessness, a new gravity was born; in place of gloom, cheerfulness appeared; Nabokumar's countenance was now ever-happy. Now that his heart was filled with love, he felt more affection for others; he grew less hostile towards those who tested his patience; he now loved every human being; it seemed to him that the world had been created only for good deeds; the whole world seemed to him a beautiful place. Such is love! Love transforms the harsh into the tender, evil into good, vice into virtue, darkness into light!

And Kapalkundala, what of her? What was her state of mind? Come, reader, let us take a look.

In Seclusion

Why, in your youth, shed all finery to wrap yourself in
    tree-bark?
Say, at dusk, can the starry, moonlit night seek out the
    sun?
Kumarsambhava

In the olden days, as we know, Saptagram was a very prosperous town. It was once a trade centre for merchants from every country, from Java to Rome. But in the tenth or eleventh century of the Bengali calendar, the ancient glory of Saptagram began to decline, mainly because the river that skirted the edge of the town had become too narrow for large vessels to navigate. As ships could no longer access the town, its flourishing business began to disappear. If a trade centre loses its business, it loses everything. Saptagram lost everything. In the eleventh century of the Bengali calendar, Hooghly, in its growing splendour, became its rival. Having begun trading in Hooghly, the

Portuguese drained the economy of Saptagram, luring away Dhanalakshmi, the town's presiding goddess of wealth. But even then, Saptagram had not entirely lost its charm. Important administrators, including military officials, still resided there; but already, many parts of the town, now ugly and abandoned, had begun to acquire a provincial air.

Nabokumar lived in an isolated suburb of the town. With Saptagram in ruins, this place now was rarely frequented by people. The main street was overrun with weeds and creepers. Just behind Nabokumar's house was a dense, extensive forest. In front of the house, almost a mile away, flowed a narrow canal, skirting a tiny field to enter the forest at the rear. The house, made of brick, was no mean structure, considering the time and place of its construction. Though double-storied, it was not unduly high: nowadays, single-storied houses are often of the same height.

On the terrace of this house stood two young women, gazing at the view. Dusk had descended. The scene that presented itself all around them was indeed a feast for the eyes. Close at hand, on one side, was a dense forest, resonant with the chirping of countless birds. Opposite the forest was the canal, narrow as a silver thread. Far away, in the distance, one could see the beautiful silhouettes of innumerable mansions, full of towns-people yearning for a touch of the fresh spring breeze. On the other side, far, far away, the darkness deepened on the immense trees that lined the shores of the river Bhagirathi, its surface adorned with boats.

Of the two young women on the terrace, one had a com-plexion like the glimmer of moonlight; she was half-concealed by her mass of unbound tresses. The other woman, dark-skinned, was a beautiful sixteen, with slender frame and tiny face, the upper portion of her countenance framed by wisps of curly hair like the petal-encircled heart of a blue lotus. Her wide eyes were pale and tender like a small saphari fish; her delicate fingers caressed her companion's wavy hair. The esteemed reader would have guessed that she of the moonlight glow was Kapalkundala. Let me add that the dark-skinned one was her nanad, her sister-in-law, Shyamasundari.

Shyamasundari addressed her sister-in-law sometimes as 'Bou' or bride, sometimes affectionately as 'Bon' or 'sister', and sometimes as 'Mrino'. Kapalkundala being such a formidable name, the family had renamed her Mrinmayi, Mrino for short. We, too, shall sometimes refer to her as Mrinmayi.

Shyamasundari was reciting a verse learnt in childhood,

The lotus-flower, she hides her face in sand,
But seeing her loved one, she blooms to attract the bee.
And the wild vine spreads her leaves to reach out to the tree;
And at flood-tide, the river-waters descend to the sea.
In moonlight blooms the flower, without being coy;
The bride sheds all restraint upon entering the nuptial bed.
What's this? A quirk of fate, for sure! How bittersweet is
    love!
Modesty forgotten, we blossom at another's touch!

'Would you remain a loner, then, in your holy pursuit of abstinence?'

'Why, what holy pursuit am I engaged in?' demanded Mrinmayi.

'Won't you braid this mass of hair?' asked Shyamasundari, lifting up Mrinmayi's wavy tresses with both hands.

With a faint smile, Mrinmayi merely pulled away the locks of hair from Shyamasundari's grasp.

'Please keep my wish,' Shyamasundari persisted. 'Dress like a housewife, just for once. How long will you remain a female ascetic – a yogini?'

'Before I met this man, descendant of Brahmins, I was indeed a yogini,' replied Kapalkundala.

'Not any more.'

'Why not?'

'Why not? Do you really want to know? I shall disrupt your holy pursuit. Do you know what a touchstone is?'

'No,' confessed Mrinmayi.

'Its touch can convert even tin to gold.'

'So what?'

'Women possess a touchstone, too.'

'What's that?'

'A man. The company of a man can turn even a yogini into a housewife. You have touched that stone. Wait and see,

I'll make you braid your hair, dress you in finery,
  Place a swaying flower-garland in your hair,
An ornament in your parting, a girdle round your waist,
  And earrings on your ears.
With kumkum, sandalwood, scent and paan-supari
  I'll tint your rosy countenance.
In your lap I'll cast a golden doll, a son,
  And we'll see if you like it or not!'

'I understand perfectly,' responded Mrinmayi. 'Let us suppose that the touchstone turns me to gold. Suppose I braid my hair, deck myself out in finery, wear flowers in my hair, a girdle round my waist, and ornaments in my ears; let us go as far as the sandalwood, kumkum, scent, paan, and even the golden doll of a son. Let us imagine it all. But even then, how will it make me happy?'

'Tell me, what about the happiness of a flower that bursts into bloom?'

'That would make people happy, but what would the flower gain from blooming?'

Shyamasundari's countenance grew grave; like blue lotuses stirred by the early morning breeze, her wide-eyed gaze wavered.

'What about the flower?' she wondered. 'I couldn't say! I have never bloomed like a flower, but had I been a bud like you, I would have blossomed with joy.

'Very well, if this does not appeal to you,' persisted Shyamasundari, when Mrinmayi remained silent, 'then tell me what makes you happy?'

'I can't say,' replied Mrinmayi, after considering for a while. 'Perhaps it would make me happy to wander in those forests by the seashore.'

Shyamasundari was surprised. She felt rather offended, even angry, at Mrinmayi's lack of gratitude towards those who had looked after her.

'How would you return there, now?' she asked.

'There can be no return.'

'Then what will you do?'

'"As I am bidden, so shall I act," the priest at the temple used to say.'

Shyamasundari covered her face with the end of her sari, stifling a smile. 'As you say, Mr Bhattacharya, sir!' she mimicked. 'So, what next?'

'Fate will determine my actions,' sighed Mrinmayi. 'Whatever destiny has in store for me, will happen.'

'Why, what could fate have in store for you? Happiness is your destiny. Why do you sigh, then?'

'Listen,' explained Mrinmayi. 'The day I set out on my journey with my husband, I offered a triple belpata at the goddess Bhavani's feet. I would never undertake any task without offering a triple leaf at Ma's lotus-like feet. If destiny decreed a positive outcome for my endeavour, Ma would accept the offering; if an inauspicious outcome was likely, the belpata would fall off her pedestal. I was apprehensive about travelling to unknown lands, accompanied by a stranger. I went to Ma for an indication of the future, to find out whether it boded ill or well for me. Ma did not accept my triple leaf offering, so I'm not sure what the future holds in store for me.'

Mrinmayi fell silent. Shyamasundari shivered.

Part 3

In the Past

The role of a servant is very painful.
Ratnavali

After Nabokumar left the chati with Kapalkundala, Motibibi changed her route and headed for Burdhwan. While she is on her way, let us recount the story of her past. Moti's character was tainted with deep sin, but also graced by great virtues. A detailed account of such a person's character will not displease the esteemed reader.

When her father converted to Islam, her Hindu name was changed to Lutfunnissa. She was not called Motibibi at all, but sometimes, she adopted that name while travelling in disguise from place to place. When he reached Dhaka, her father entered royal service. But the place was frequented by many people from his own region. After having lost their social position, not everyone would like to continue in their original place of domicile. Hence, having gradually gained the favour of the subedar, he obtained letters of reference from numerous rich umraos and moved to Agra with his family. No person of talent could fail to attract Emperor Akbar's attention. He soon took note of this gentleman's expertise. In a short time, Lutfunnissa's father rose in the ranks to become one of the chief umraos of Agra.

Meanwhile, Lutfunnissa was growing up. In Agra, she became well-versed in Persian, Sanskrit, dance, music and the arts. She was ranked foremost among the innumerable beautiful and talented women of Agra. Unfortunately, her training in religious matters did not match her expertise in learned subjects. As she grew up, she began to display a wild, uncontrollable temperament. She had neither the ability, nor the inclination, to curb her sensuous appetites. When it came to questions of morality, it was exactly the same. She did exactly as she pleased, without first considering the rightness or wrongness of an action. She performed good deeds and evil deeds as it pleased her heart. Her nature developed the flaws that appear when youthful instincts run wild, without control. As her former husband was alive, none of the umraos, royal courtiers, were willing to marry her. She, too, showed no particular desire for marriage. 'Why clip the wings of the bee that flits from flower to flower?' she thought, in her heart of hearts. At first there were rumours, then, ultimately, scandal. Her father threw her out of the house in disgust.

Crown Prince Selim was one of the secret recipients of Lutfunnissa's favours. Selim, until now, had not made Lutfunnissa part of his harem, for fear of incurring the wrath of his impartial father if this unchaste woman brought family dishonour upon one of the umraos. Now, he found his opportunity. The sister of the Rajput king Raja Mansingh was the Crown Prince's chief consort. The Crown Prince appointed Lutfunnissa her chief companion. Officially, Lutfunnissa was the Begum's companion, but in private, she became a beneficiary of the Crown Prince's largesse.

As we can easily imagine, a clever woman like Lutfunnissa quickly won the prince's heart. So completely did she dominate his affections, eliminating all competition, that she developed a firm resolve to become his reigning queen at the appropriate time. This was not only Lutfunnissa's own resolve; everyone in the royal palace also perceived this as a likely possibility. Lutfunnissa passed her days, rapt in these rosy dreams, when all of a sudden, she was rudely awakened. Mehrunnissa, daughter of Khaja Ayesh, treasurer to Emperor Akbar, was the reigning beauty of the Muslim community. One day, the treasurer invited Prince Selim to his home, along with other eminent personages. That day, Selim met Mehrunnissa, and gave her his heart. What happened thereafter is well known to readers of history. The treasurer's daughter was already betrothed to a very powerful umrao named Sher Afghan. Blinded by love, Selim beseeched his father to break that engagement, but all he received was a scolding from his fair-minded parent. For the time being, Selim had to desist, but he did not give up hope. Sher Afghan married Mehrunnissa. But Lutfunnissa understood all the nuances of Selim's psychology. She knew for sure that there would be no escape for Sher Afghan, even if he was blessed with a thousand lives. As soon as Emperor Akbar passed away, Sher Afghan would die, and Mehrunnissa would become Selim's queen. Lutfunnissa gave up her designs on the throne.

Akbar, the pride of the reigning Muslim dynasty, reached the end of his lifespan. The sun that had irradiated the entire region from Turkey to the Brahmaputra, was now about to set. At this time, to preserve her position of eminence, Lutfunnissa made a daring resolve.

The Rajput ruler Raja Mansingh's sister was Selim's chief consort. Khusrau was her son. One day, in the course of a discussion with her about Emperor Akbar's illness, Lutfunnissa congratulated her on the prospect of a Rajput's daughter becoming the reigning queen.

'A woman may indeed consider her life worthwhile if she becomes the Emperor's wife, but the Emperor's mother is senior to all,' retorted Khusrau's mother.

A novel strategy immediately suggested itself to Lutfunnissa's mind.

'Why not?' she responded. 'That, too, is within your control.'

'How is that?' wondered the Begum.

'Give the throne to Khusrau, the Crown Prince's son!' proposed the clever woman.

The Begum did not reply. The matter was not mentioned again that day, but neither of them forgot it. The Begum was not averse to the idea that her son, rather than her husband, should ascend the throne; Selim's infatuation with Mehrunnissa was as much a thorn in the flesh for her, as it was for Lutfunnissa. Why should Mansingh's sister take kindly to the idea of being ordered about by an upstart, daughter of a Turk? Lutfunnissa also had her own secret reasons for aiding and abetting this plan. The matter was raised again, another day. The two of them came to an agreement.

It did not seem impossible to dismiss Selim, in order to establish Khusrau on Akbar's throne. Lutfunnissa took great pains to convince the Begum of this.

'The Mughal empire is sustained by the might of the Rajputs,' she argued. 'Raja Mansingh, the leading light of the Rajput clan, is Khusrau's mama, his maternal uncle; and Khan Azim, leader of the Muslims and chief minister to the Emperor, is Khusrau's father-in-law; if these two men are ready to accept the arrangement, who would not follow them? And with whose support would the Crown Prince ascend the throne? It is your responsibility to commit Raja Mansingh to this undertaking. It is mine, to enlist the support of Khan Azim and the other Muslim umraos. With your blessings, I shall succeed, but I fear that Khusrau, having ascended the throne, might expel this errant woman from the fort.'

The Begum understood her companion's intentions.

'You will be accepted by any umrao in Agra whose wife you wish to become,' she smiled. 'Your husband will become a royal official on a salary of five thousand.'

Lutfunnissa was satisfied. This, indeed, had been her motive. What joy in clipping the wings of the bee that flitted from flower to flower, to live in the royal palace as a humble housewife? If freedom must be surrendered, what pleasure would she derive from being slave to Mehrunnissa, her childhood playmate? It would be more glorious by far, to marry some important royal functionary, to become the centre of his existence.

It was not merely this temptation that spurred Lutfunnissa to adopt such a course of action. She also wanted to avenge herself because Selim had ignored her and showered all his attention on Mehrunnissa.

Khan Azim and the other umraos of Agra and Delhi were very much under Lutfunnissa's thumb. It was hardly surprising that Khan Azim should promote the interests of his son-in-law. He and the other umraos agreed to the plan.

'Suppose things go wrong and our plot does not succeed?' Khan Azim urged Lutfunnissa. 'There will be no saving us then. So, it's best to devise some means of saving our lives.'

'What would you advise?'

'There is no refuge but Orissa,' Khan Azim declared. 'That is the only place where the hold of the Mughal administration is weak. It is necessary to have the Orissa army within our control. Your brother is an official in Orissa; tomorrow, I shall spread word that he has been injured in battle. On the pretext of going to see him, you must leave for Orissa tomorrow itself. Come back as soon as your mission there is accomplished.'

Lutfunnissa consented to this proposal. The esteemed reader has encountered her on her journey back from Orissa.

Change of Route

We fall to the ground but rise again, with the earth's
    support;
Whoever dies of despair at a single blow of misfortune?
The storm has brought me low but I shall not give up
    hope;
Though thwarted today, my efforts may bear fruit
    tomorrow.

Nabin Tapaswini

Having taken leave of Nabokumar, Motibibi, alias Lutfunnissa, set out for Burdhwan, but she could not reach her destination on the same day. She spent the night at a different chati. That evening, she chatted with Peshaman.

'Peshaman! What did you think of my husband?' Motibibi suddenly wanted to know.

'Why, what should I think of him?' asked Peshaman, rather surprised.

'Isn't he handsome?'

Peshaman had developed a special aversion to Nabokumar. She had once coveted the ornaments that Motibibi had given Kapalkundala, hoping that one day the jewels would be hers for the asking. But now that this hope had been shattered, Peshaman felt a tremendous hostility towards Kapalkundala and her husband.

Hence, she replied: 'How can one think of an impoverished Brahmin as either handsome or ugly?'

'If the impoverished Brahmin becomes an umrao, would he not appear handsome?' laughed Moti, sensing her companion's mood.

'What's that supposed to mean?'

'Why, don't you know the Begum has agreed to appoint my husband as an umrao if Khusrau becomes Emperor?'

'I know that, indeed. But why should your former husband become an umrao?'

'What other husband do I have?'

'Your husband-to-be.'

'Two husbands for a chaste woman like me? What an impertinent thought!' protested Moti with a faint smile. 'Who goes there?' she called out suddenly.

Peshaman recognised the person in question as a resident of Agra, a trusted member of Khan Azim's entourage. The two women grew agitated. Peshaman called out to the man.

Approaching them, he greeted Lutfunnissa and handed her a letter.

'I was carrying this letter to Orissa,' he told her. 'It's very urgent.'

Motibibi's hopes evaporated as she read the letter. This was what it said,

> Our efforts have been fruitless. Even at the time of his death, Akbar Shah has defeated us with his intelligence. He has now left us for his heavenly abode. By his orders, Prince Selim has become Jehangir Shah, the Emperor. Please do not worry about Khusrau. To ensure that no one acts against you in this matter, please return to Agra as fast as possible.

How Akbar Shah handled this conspiracy, history books have recounted; there is no need to go into those details here.

Having dismissed the messenger with a tip, Moti read the letter aloud to Peshaman.

'What should we do now?' wondered Peshaman.

'There's nothing we can do now,' replied Moti.

'Well, what harm in that?' pronounced Peshaman, after some thought. 'You may as well continue as before, for any woman who belongs to the royal establishment enjoys more importance than even the reigning queen of some other state.'

'That's not possible anymore,' Moti explained, with a faint smile. 'I can no longer remain in that palace. Jehangir will waste no time in marrying Mehrunnissa. I have known Mehrunnissa since adolescence. Once she enters the palace, she will become the emperor, and Jehangir will remain Badshah only in name. She will discover that I had tried to obstruct her path to the throne. What will be my fate, then?'

'What will happen, now?' Peshaman was almost in tears.

'There is only one hope. What are Mehrunnissa's feelings for Jehangir? Such is her firmness of character, that if she cares more for her husband than for Jehangir, then she will not surrender her heart to Jehangir even if he were to murder a hundred Sher Afghans. But if Mehrunnissa is genuinely in love with Jehangir, then there is no hope for us.'

'How will you discover the secrets of Mehrunnissa's heart?'

'What can Lutfunnissa not accomplish?' smiled Moti. 'Mehrunnissa is my childhood companion. Tomorrow, I shall set out for Burdhwan, to spend a couple of days with her.'

'If Mehrunnissa is in love with the Badshah, what will you do?'

'My father used to say: "The situation will determine our course of action."'

For a while, they were silent. A faint smile began to play upon Moti's lips.

'Why do you smile?' asked Peshaman.

'A new idea has occurred to me.'

'What is it?'

Moti did not tell Peshaman what it was. We, too, shall withhold it from the reader. Eventually, the truth will reveal itself.

In the Rival's Home

Shyam alone, and none but he, rules over my heart.
Uddhavduta

At this time, Sher Afghan was the official in charge of the Burdhwan administration, under the authority of the Subedar of Bengal. Having arrived at Burdhwan, Motibibi presented herself at his house. Sher Afghan, along with his family, welcomed her warmly as a household guest. When Sher Afghan and his wife Mehrunnissa were residents of Agra, Moti had been one of their close acquaintances, particularly intimate with Mehrunnissa. Afterwards, the two of them had become rivals in their designs upon the throne of Delhi.

'Which of us is destined to rule India?' Mehrunnissa wondered, now that they were reunited. 'Only Fate knows the answer, and Selim; and if anyone else is in the know, it would be Lutfunnissa. Let's see if Lutfunnissa has anything to reveal!'

Motibibi, too, was trying to decipher Mehrunnissa's frame of mind.

At that time, Mehrunnissa was renowned as the most beautiful and talented woman in India. Indeed, very few women like her have been born into this world. Every historian has acknowledged her prominent place amongst the legendary beauties of this world. Among the men of her time, few could match her at any skill. Her talent for music and dance was unparalleled; in poetry and the visual arts as well, she could hold her audience enthralled. Her gift for conversation was even more captivating than her physical beauty. In all these aspects, Moti, too, was in no way less talented. These two enchantresses were now keen to understand each other's minds.

Mehrunnissa was in the special parlour, painting a picture. Peering over her shoulder was Lutfunnissa, chewing paan, betel leaf, as she watched her paint.

'What do you think of my painting?' asked Mehrunnissa.

'It is typical of your artistry. It's a pity nobody else can boast of your artistic skills.'

'If that is indeed true, then why is it a pity?'

'If others had your artistic talent, they could paint your image as a keepsake.'

'In my grave, my image will be entombed.'

Mehrunnissa pronounced these words with gravity.

'My sister!' cried Moti. 'Why are you in such low spirits, today?'

'Low spirits? Of course not! But how can I forget that you leave at dawn tomorrow? Why should you not gratify me by staying a couple of days longer?'

'Who doesn't fancy a life of pleasure? Would I leave, if I had my way? But I must act as others decree: how can I linger here?'

'You don't love me anymore, else you would have extended your stay. If you could travel to this place, why can't you stay on?'

'I have told you everything. My brother, a mansabdar in the Mughal army, was grievously injured in a skirmish with the Pathans of Orissa. When I received tidings of his condition, I travelled to this region to visit him, with the Begum's permission. I have spent too much time in Orissa, but now I should delay no more. I spent these two days with you because we had not met for a very long time.'

'By which date have you promised the Begum that you will return?'

Moti realised that Mehrunnissa was being sarcastic. She could not match Mehrunnissa in the art of polished, yet piercing irony. But she, too, was never at a loss for words.

'Is it possible to fix a date when embarking on a three-month-long journey? But I have delayed too long; any further delay might incur displeasure.'

'Whose displeasure do you fear?' inquired Mehrunnissa with her captivating smile. 'The Crown Prince's, or his consort's?'

'Would you embarrass me, shameless person that I am?' responded Moti, slightly discomfited. 'Both could be displeased.'

'But why not assume the title of Begum yourself, may I ask? I hear that Prince Selim is to marry you, as his special consort. How far have those plans advanced?'

'I am easily subjugated. Why should I surrender the little freedom I have? As the Begum's companion, I could easily travel to Orissa; but as Selim's Begum, could I have done the same?'

'For one who will be the reigning queen of Delhi, what need to travel to Orissa?'

'I would never dare aspire to become Selim's reigning queen. In Hindustan, only Mehrunnissa is fit to reign supreme over the heart of Delhi's ruler.'

Mehrunnissa lowered her head. 'My sister!' she pleaded, after a short silence, 'I shall not try to ascertain whether you uttered these words to hurt my feelings, or to know my mind. But when you speak to me, I beg you not to forget that I am Sher Afghan's wife, his devoted slave in body, mind and soul.'

Far from being put out by this admonition, the brazen Moti took this opportunity to advance her argument.

'That you are a devoted wife, I know only too well,' she persisted. 'That is why I have dared to raise this subject indirectly. My aim is to make you aware that Selim has been unable to forget the magic of your beauty. Please remain careful.'

'Now I understand. But what have I to fear?'

'Widowhood,' declared Moti, after some hesitation.

As she spoke, Moti fixed her gaze upon Mehrunnissa's countenance, but could detect no trace of fear or joy.

'Fear of widowhood!' cried Mehrunnissa proudly. 'Sher Afghan is not incapable of protecting himself! Under the rule of Akbar Shah, even the emperor's own son would not be spared if he destroyed an innocent life.'

'True, indeed. But according to the latest news from Agra, Akbar Shah is no more. Selim has ascended the throne. Who can stop the monarch of Delhi?'

Mehrunnissa said no more. Tremors shook her entire body. Once more she lowered her head; tears flowed from her eyes.

'Why do you weep?' asked Moti.

'Selim enthroned as the emperor of India, and what about me?' sighed Mehrunnissa.

Moti's purpose was fulfilled.

'Have you not been able to forget the Crown Prince completely, even now?' she enquired.

'Forget? Who am I supposed to forget?' cried Mehrunnissa, in a choking voice. 'I may forget my own life, but I can never forget the Crown Prince. But listen, my sister! I have suddenly opened the doors of my heart to you. You have heard what I just said, but by my word, let this matter not reach the ears of any other person.'

'Very well, so it shall be,' promised Moti. 'But when Selim hears of my visit to Burdhwan, he will certainly want to know what Mehrunnissa had to say about him. How shall I answer him then?'

'Tell him that Mehrunnissa will dwell upon his image, which she cherishes in her heart,' instructed Mehrunnissa, after some thought. 'She will give up her life for him, if necessary. But she will never sacrifice her family honour. As long as her husband, her lord and master, remains alive, this humble slave will never show her face to the emperor of Delhi. And if her husband's death is engineered by the monarch of Delhi, then she will never give herself to her husband's murderer, not as long as she lives.'

With these words, Mehrunnissa left the room. Motibibi gazed after her in wonder. But the victory was Motibibi's. She had fathomed the state of Mehrunnissa's heart, but Mehrunnissa had not understood Motibibi's hopes and plans at all. Even she – the woman who, by dint of her own intelligence, would rule the heart of Delhi's ruler – was outwitted by Motibibi. This was because Mehrunnissa was a woman in love, while Motibibi, in this instance, was guided solely by self-interest.

Motibibi was familiar with the vagaries of the human heart. The conclusions she drew after considering Mehrunnissa's words, proved in time to be entirely accurate. She realised that Mehrunnissa was genuinely in love with Jehangir; whatever she may say now in a spirit of womanly pride, she would not be able to restrain her wayward heart once the path was clear. She would surely submit to the Emperor's desires.

Having reached this conclusion, Moti's hopes and dreams evaporated. But did this cast her into a state of extreme grief? Not at all! In fact, she felt rather happy. At first, Moti could not understand why this impossible joy should arise in her heart. She headed for Agra. The journey took a few days. During that time, she became acquainted with her own state of mind.

At the Royal Palace

Think not of me as your wife, henceforth.
Birangana Kavya

Moti arrived in Agra. There is no need to refer to her as Moti anymore, for in a few days, her attitudes and inclinations had been utterly transformed.

She met Jehangir. He welcomed her with warmth, as before, asking after her brother's health and hoping she had had a good journey. What Lutfunnissa had predicted to Mehrunnissa proved true. After some desultory conversation, the subject of Burdhwan came up.

'You say you spent a couple of days with Mehrunnissa; what did she say about me?' enquired Jehangir.

Artlessly, Lutfunnissa told him about Mehrunnissa's love for him. The Emperor listened in silence; a few tears fell from his wide-open eyes.

'My lord!' beseeched Lutfunnissa, 'Your humble slave has brought you good tidings. But you have not yet announced a reward for her.'

'Bibi! Your desires are limitless!' laughed the Emperor.

'My lord! How is your humble slave to blame?'

'I have made the Badshah of Delhi your vassal, and you still want more rewards?'

'Women have many desires,' laughed Lutfunnissa.

'What is your latest desire?'

'Let Your Highness declare, first, that this humble slave's plea will be granted.'

'Yes, if it does not hamper the process of governance.'

'A single person cannot hamper the official work of the Emperor of Delhi,' smiled Lutfunnissa.

'In that case, I consent. Tell us what it is you desire.'

'I fancy getting married.'

'A novel desire, indeed!' guffawed Jehangir. 'Has a match been fixed?'

'Indeed it has. We only await your royal consent. Without the Emperor's consent, no match can be finalised.'

'What need of my consent? Who is this man you intend to sweep away on this tide of joy?'

'Your humble slave may have served the emperor of Delhi, but that doesn't make her an unfaithful woman. Your slave wants permission to marry her own husband.'

'Is that so, indeed! And what will be the fate of yours truly, your old retainer?'

'As a parting gift, I shall present to you Mehrunnissa, empress of Delhi.'

'Who is Mehrunnissa, empress of Delhi?'

'She is the empress-to-be.'

Privately, Jehangir took this to mean that Lutfunnissa considered it inevitable that Mehrunnissa would become empress of Delhi. Her heart's desire thwarted, she seemed to be seeking release from her confinement in the royal establishment, because it no longer held any charm for her. Hurt at what he inferred to be her mindset, Jehangir remained silent.

'Does Your Highness object to this proposal?' urged Lutfunnissa.

'I have no objection. But why must you remarry your husband?'

'The first time we were married, my husband did not accept me as his wife – such was my misfortune. This time, he cannot reject Your Highness' humble slave.'

The Badshah laughed merrily, then grew grave.

'My love!' he said, 'There is nothing I would not grant you. If you are so inclined, please act accordingly. But why must you leave me? Don't the sun and moon inhabit the same sky? Can't two flowers bloom on the same stalk?'

'That may be true of tiny flowers, but one stem cannot support two lotuses,' answered Lutfunnissa, fixing her wide gaze upon the Badshah. 'Why should I remain a thorn beneath your bejewelled throne?'

Lutfunnissa returned to her own quarters. She had not revealed to Jehangir the reasons underlying her heart's desire. Jehangir was satisfied with what he could sense about her feelings from her behaviour. He understood nothing of the deep, concealed facts of the matter. Lutfunnissa's heart was made of stone. Even Selim's royal bearing, which won the hearts of women, had failed to captivate her. But now, a worm had found its way into the stone.

In the temple of the Self

A lifetime of gazing at his beauty, and my eyes haven't
   had their fill;
Hearing his sweet words, my ears still crave the sound
   of his voice.

So many tender nights together, but my heart desires
   him still;
For a thousand centuries I held him in my heart, yet
   I have no peace.
Vidyapati says, of all the interesting men in this world,
Not one in a million is as enchanting as he.

Vidyapati

Back home, Lutfunnissa cheerfully sent for Peshaman and discarded her finery.

'You may have this costume,' she told Peshaman, removing her gold-and-pearl-encrusted attire.

Peshaman was rather surprised. The outfit had been stitched very recently, at great expense.

'Why are you giving me this dress?' she asked. 'What's the news?'

'Good news, indeed,' replied Lutfunnissa.

'That is obvious. Have you overcome your apprehensions regarding Mehrunnissa?'

'I have. We have no cause for worry on that account.'

'So that makes me the Begum's handmaiden!' exclaimed Peshaman, overjoyed.

'If you wish to be the Begum's handmaiden, I shall refer you to Mehrunnissa.'

'What's this you say? But you tell me there is no likelihood of Mehrunnissa becoming the Badshah's Begum.'

'I told you nothing of the sort. I said I was not worried on that account.'

'Isn't there cause for worry? If you don't become sole empress of Agra, all is lost.'

'I shall sever all links with Agra.'

'What's that supposed to mean? I can't make head or tail of all this. Please explain today's glad tidings to me.'

'The glad news is that I am leaving Agra for good.'

'Where will you go?'

'I shall move to Bengal. If possible, I shall marry a gentleman, a bhadralok.'

'Such sarcasm is novel, indeed, but it sets my heart atremble.'

'I'm not joking. I am really leaving Agra for good. I have taken leave of the Emperor.'

'What made you think of such a terrible idea?'

'It is not a bad idea. I had such a long sojourn in Agra, but to what avail? Ever since I was a child, I had an intense thirst for happiness. To quench that thirst, I travelled here, all the way from Bengal. To obtain that precious jewel, was there any fortune I would not squander, any sin I would not commit? And as for my aims in going to such lengths, was there any purpose that I failed to accomplish? Wealth, property, riches, glory, prestige – I have enjoyed all these in abundance, after all. But ultimately, what did I gain for all my efforts? As I sit here, recapitulating all those days, I can declare that I never enjoyed any happiness, not for a single day, not even for a single moment. I never felt fulfilled; my craving only continued to grow. I can attain even greater wealth and property if I make the effort, but to what end? If these things were a source of happiness, then in all these days, I would have found happiness at least once, just for a single day. This desire for happiness is like a mountain waterfall; it emerges at first from a desolate place, as a pure, narrow stream, concealed in its own womb, unbeknownst to all, babbling to itself, unheard by anyone. The further it flows, the wider and murkier it becomes. Sometimes, the wind blows, too, generating waves; crocodiles and makaras come to inhabit the waters. The stream expands, grows even more muddy and salty; countless sandbanks and deserts appear upon the river's bosom; its pace slackens. Where this murky river-body will find a place to hide in the endless ocean now, who can tell?'

'I haven't understood any of this. Why do you not find happiness in such things?'

'I have at last realised why these things don't make me happy. In a single night, on my way back from Orissa, I experienced the happiness I could not find in the three years that I have spent in the shadow of this royal palace. This has made me realise the truth.'

'What have you realised?'

'All this while, I was like a Hindu idol, outwardly embellished with gold and jewels, but inwardly, made of stone. I have braved the fires of worldly life, seeking the pleasures of the senses, but the flames have never touched me. Now let me see if I can search within the stone to find a heart made of flesh and blood.'

'I don't understand any of this, either.'

'Have I ever loved anyone here, in Agra?'

'No one at all!' whispered Peshaman.

'Am I not a woman with a heart of stone, then?'

'Well, why don't you fall in love now, if you so desire?'

'That is indeed my desire. That's why I am leaving Agra.'

'What need of that? Is there a dearth of people in Agra that you should turn to a region full of scoundrels? Why not love the Badshah himself, now, if he loves you? When it comes to appearance, wealth, splendour, or what you will, is there anyone in the world who can surpass the Badshah of Delhi?'

'Why does water flow downwards when the moon and stars are in the sky above?'

'Why?'

'It's destiny.'

Lutfunnissa did not disclose the entire truth. The fire had made its way into the stone, which was dissolving in the heat.

Obeisance

Body, mind and heart, to you I surrender;
Enjoy a royal feast at your female slave's abode.
Birangana Kavya

When seeds are sown in the field, they sprout of their own accord. Nobody can sense, or witness, their sprouting. Once the seed is sown, wherever its planter might be, it gradually grows from a seedling into a tree. Today, the plant might be tiny, finger-sized, escaping the beholder's eye. Then, little by little, it grows, until it is a foot and a half, then a yard in height. Still, if it does not seem useful to anyone's selfish needs, it is overlooked even when it is within sight. Days pass, then months and years; gradually, it begins to catch the eye. There is no ignoring it now: slowly, the tree grows taller, its shadow destroying other trees, until no other vegetation can survive in that field.

Lutfunnissa's love had expanded in the same way. First, there was the sudden encounter with her beloved. At that moment, the seed of love was sown, though she was not particularly aware of it. Afterwards, she did not meet him again. But, in his absence, she repeatedly recalled his face, taking pleasure in conjuring up his image in her memory. The seedling sprouted. She began to love that image. It is a law of human nature that the oftener we perform a mental task, the more we relish it; eventually, such activity acquires the semblance of a natural, inborn trait. Day and night, Lutfunnissa began to nurture that image in her heart. She felt a desperate urge to see him; it now became hard to control her natural desires. Even the temptation of capturing the throne of Delhi seemed less important in comparison. The throne seemed to her to be encircled with flames produced by the arrows of Manmatha, god of love. Throwing kingdom, capital and royal throne to the winds, she rushed to meet her beloved. The man she loved was Nabokumar.

This was why even the disclosures of Mehrunnissa, which sounded the death knell to her own aspirations, had not made Lutfunnissa downcast; this was why, upon her return to Agra, she made no effort to safeguard what was hers; why she took leave of the Badshah forever.

Lutfunnissa arrived in Saptagram. She took up residence in a mansion within the city, not far from the highway. Travellers on the road noticed that the mansion was suddenly full of servants in gold-trimmed livery. The decor in every room was exquisite. Fragrant substances, sprayed perfume and flower petals were scattered everywhere with gay abandon. Gold and silver decorations, inlaid with ivory, brightened every corner of the mansion. In one such ornate chamber sat Lutfunnissa, with lowered countenance; opposite her, on a separate mat, was Nabokumar. Lutfunnissa had met Nabokumar in Saptagram a couple of times before this; their conversation on this present occasion will reveal the extent to which those earlier meetings had helped Lutfunnissa attain her ends.

'I shall take your leave, then,' said Nabokumar after a short silence. 'Please don't send for me again.'

'Please don't go!' pleaded Lutfunnissa. 'Stay a little longer. I haven't finished what I had to say.'

Nabokumar waited, but Lutfunnissa did not continue.

'What else do you have to say?' asked Nabokumar after a while.

Lutfunnissa did not reply. Observing that she was weeping silently, Nabokumar rose to his feet. Lutfunnissa clutched at the end of his garment.

'Tell me, what is the matter?' demanded Nabokumar, rather irritated.

'What do you want?' asked Lutfunnissa. 'Is there nothing in the world that you desire? Wealth, property, prestige, love, amusement, mystery – I offer you all the things that are associated with happiness in this life, expecting nothing in return. I only want to be your slave. I don't ask for the privilege of becoming your wife, I only want to be your slave!'

'I am a poor Brahmin,' replied Nabokumar. 'And in this life, a poor Brahmin I shall remain. I cannot accept your gifts of wealth and property, to become the paramour of a Yavanakanya, daughter of a different faith.'

Paramour of a Yavanakanya! Nabokumar was not aware, even now, that this woman was his own wife. Lutfunnissa hung her head. Nabokumar extricated the end of his garment from her grasp.

'Very well, then, let it be!' cried Lutfunnissa, clutching at the corner of his dhoti once more. 'If the Lord so desires, let me drown all my longings and inclinations in the bottomless deep. I ask nothing more of you, but that sometimes, you will pass this way. Think me your slave and appear to me now and then, so I can merely feast my eyes upon you!'

'You are a Yavani, a woman of a different faith, and wife of another man. Even this mode of interaction with you would be sinful. We shall never meet again.'

There was a short silence. A storm raged in Lutfunnissa's heart. Like an image carved in stone, she remained immobile. Then she released the corner of Nabokumar's dhoti.

'Go!' she said.

Nabokumar turned to leave. He had barely walked a few paces, when, like a storm-uprooted plant, Lutfunnissa cast herself at his feet.

'O heartless one!' she cried, twining her arms, vine-like, around his ankles. 'For your sake, I gave up the throne of Agra to come here. Please don't abandon me!'

'Please go back to Agra,' Nabokumar insisted. 'As for me, you may as well give up hope.'

'Not as long as I live!' declared Lutfunnissa proudly, springing to her feet, swift as an arrow. 'As long as I live, I shall not give up hope of receiving your love.'

Head held high, neck slightly arched, with her unflinching gaze fixed on Nabokumar's countenance, stood the woman who had stolen the heart of the king of kings. The inflexible pride that had melted in the flames of passion, again shone forth; the invincible strength of mind that had remained undaunted at the prospect of governing the Indian empire, was again restored to her person, which love had earlier made weak. The veins in her forehead swelled, in an exquisite tracery of lines; her bright eyes glittered like the ocean's surface in sunlight; her nostrils quivered. As a swan frolicking in the river current arches her neck to confront the one who obstructs her play, as a snake raises her hood to strike the one who has trodden upon her head, so stood this wild, enraged Yavani, poised, with her head held high.

'Not as long as I live!' she declared. 'You shall be mine alone.'

The vision of this woman, so like a ferocious serpent, frightened Nabokumar. Lutfunnissa's indescribable voluptuousness struck him as never before. But the magic of that beauty was like a flash of lightning, predicting thunder; it was a sight to terrify the soul. About to leave, Nabokumar suddenly recalled the image of a fiery-spirited woman. One day, annoyed with his first wife Padmabati, he had threatened to expel her from the bedroom. The twelve-year-old girl had then turned upon him, her posture exuding fierce pride; just so, her eyes had flashed fire; just so, the veins in her forehead had swelled; just so had her nostrils quivered; just so had she tilted her head. It was ages since he had recalled this image; but now it came to mind. The resemblance seemed exact.

'Who are you?' asked Nabokumar slowly, in a halting voice, his heart assailed with doubt.

The pupils in the Yavani's eyes grew even more dilated.

'I am Padmabati!'

Without waiting for a reply, Lutfunnissa swept out of the room. Troubled and preoccupied, Nabokumar made his way home.

On the Outskirts of the City

…I am settled, and bend up,
Each corporal agent to this terrible feat
Macbeth

Rushing into another chamber, Lutfunnissa bolted the door. For two days, she did not emerge. In these two days, she determined what she should do and what she must avoid. Having decided upon her course of action, she was firm in her resolve. The sun was declining as Lutfunnissa, aided by Peshaman, began to dress. What an extraordinary costume! There was no trace of the feminine in her attire.

'Tell me, Peshaman, am I recognisable?' she asked, inspecting her clothes in the mirror.

'Who would recognise you now?'

'I'll be on my way, then. Let no attendants accompany me.'

'Please forgive your humble slave's impertinence, but may I ask a question?' asked Peshaman, rather hesitantly.

'What is it?'

'What purpose do you have in mind?'

'Kapalkundala's permanent separation from her husband, to begin with. Afterwards, he shall be mine.'

'Bibi! Please think carefully. The woods are dense, it's almost dark, and you will be all alone.'

Without offering any reply, Lutfunnissa left the house. She headed for the desolate, forested outskirts of Saptagram, where Nabokumar lived. It grew dark by the time she got there. The esteemed reader may recall the deep forest not far from Nabokumar's home. Having reached the edge of that forest, she rested beneath a tree. For a while, she thought about the daring plan she had set out to execute. As it happened, help arrived in an unprecedented form.

From her resting place, Lutfunnissa could hear a continuous, monotonous sound emitted by a human voice. Rising to her feet and looking all about her, she saw a light within the forest. Lutfunnissa was braver than a man; she advanced towards the light. First, she observed the scene from behind a tree, to ascertain the situation. The light, she realised, came from the flames of a sacrificial fire; the sound she had heard was the chanting of a prayer. Listening to the words of the prayer, she recognised one word for a name. As soon as she heard that name, Lutfunnissa went up to the person performing the ritual, and took her place beside him.

There let her remain, for the present. It has been a long time since the esteemed reader received news of Kapalkundala; we must now offer him some information about her.

Part 4

Inside the Bedchamber

Break, I beseech you, the shackles that bind Radhika!
Brajangana Kavya

It had taken Lutfunnissa almost a year to travel to Agra, and
thence to Saptagram. For over a year, Kapalkundala had been
Nabokumar's wife. That evening, while Lutfunnissa wandered
in the forest, Kapalkundala rested in her bedroom, in rather an
absent frame of mind. This was not the same Kapalkundala –
unadorned, with flowing, unbound tresses – whom the esteemed
reader had encountered on the seashore. Shyamasundari's
prediction had come true; the magic of the touchstone had transformed the female ascetic into a housewife. Those heavy locks,
cascading to her ankles in intricate coils like countless gleaming
black serpents, were now confined in a heavy braid down her
back. Even the braid was artfully contrived, her fine, ornamental
hairstyle revealing Shyamasundari's expert touch. Nor had
flower-garlands been forgotten, for they were twined about her
hair, encircling the braid like a crown. The locks of hair that
escaped the braid did not lie smoothly; in clusters of curls, they
graced her head in fine, black, wavy lines. Her countenance, no
longer half-concealed by heavy tresses, was now visible in all its
glowing beauty, touched only in places by tiny tendrils of hair
with beads of moisture on them. Her complexion still resembled
the glimmer of moonbeams on a half-moon night. Gold earrings
dangled at her earlobes now, a diamond necklace graced her
throat. Her ornaments did not appear faded against the brightness of her complexion; they were like the nocturnal blossoms
that grace the moonlight-enshrouded lap of the earth on a half-
moon night. She was attired in white, the pale fabric resembling
the flimsy white clouds that adorn the sky in the light of the crescent moon. Her complexion still glowed like the crescent moon,

but appeared somewhat dimmer than before, as if dark clouds had appeared somewhere on the horizon.

Kapalkundala was not alone. She was engaged in conversation with her companion Shyamasundari. The esteemed reader must overhear part of their exchange.

'How long will our Thakurjamai, your husband, remain here?' Kapalkundala wanted to know.

'He leaves tomorrow,' Shyamasundari replied. 'Ah! If only I had plucked the medicinal herb tonight, I could still have cast my spell upon him and fulfilled all my life's desires. But after being chastised for venturing out of doors last night, how can I step out again tonight?'

'Can't you pluck it in the daytime?'

'How would it work if plucked in the daytime? One must pluck it exactly at midnight, with one's hair unbound. Well, my friend, my innermost desire must remain buried in my heart.'

'But this morning, I have identified the herb, and also the place where it grows in the forest. There is no need for you to venture out tonight; I shall go and fetch the herb alone.'

'Once is enough. There's no need for you to go out again at night.'

'Why worry on that account? Haven't you heard that nocturnal wandering is my childhood habit? Just think, but for that habit of mine, you and I would never have set eyes upon each other.'

'I am afraid to speak of that. But is it a good idea for the wives and daughters of gentlefolk to wander alone in the woods at night? Considering the chastisement I had to suffer even when the two of us went out together, would there be any saving you if you went out alone?'

'What's the harm? Do you, too, believe that the simple act of going out at night will make a loose woman of me?'

'I don't believe that. But wicked people will say wicked things.'

'Let them say what they will. That won't make me a wicked person.'

'Indeed it won't. But if people speak ill of you, it will hurt our feelings deeply.'

'Don't let such unjust aspersions hurt your feelings.'

'That, too, I can handle. But why make Dada, my elder brother, unhappy?'

Kapalkundala glanced obliquely at Shyamasundari with her bright, tender eyes. 'If it makes him unhappy, how can I help it?' she said. 'Had I known that marriage, for a woman, means slavery, I would never have married at all.'

Shyamasundari thought it best to say no more. She went away to resume her household duties.

Kapalkundala busied herself with essential domestic chores. The housework done, she went out in search of the medicinal herb. The hour was late. It was a moonlit night. From his window in the outer chamber, Nabokumar saw Kapalkundala leave the house. Stepping outside, he caught her by the arm.

'What is the matter?' asked Kapalkundala.

'Where are you going?' There was no trace of admonition in his voice.

'Shyamasundari wants to seduce her husband with the help of a medicinal herb. I am going in search of the herb.'

'Fine, but you had gone out last night, too, hadn't you?' asked Nabokumar, his tone as gentle as before. 'Why again, tonight?'

'Last night, I couldn't find the herb. I shall search again tonight.'

'Very well, but couldn't you search in the daytime?' suggested Nabokumar, very softly, his voice full of tenderness.

'The medicine doesn't work in the daytime.'

'Why must you hunt for the medicine? Tell me the name of the herb. I shall fetch it for you.'

'I recognise the plant, but I don't know its name. And it won't work if you pluck it. A woman must pluck it, with her hair undone. Please don't hinder me when I try to help another.'

Kapalkundala sounded offended. Nabokumar raised no more objections.

'Let's go,' he said. 'I shall accompany you.'

'Come, see for yourself whether I am unfaithful or not!' retorted Kapalkundala proudly.

Nabokumar was silenced. With a sigh, he relinquished Kapalkundala's arm and went back into the house. Kapalkundala entered the forest alone.

In the Woods

Tender is the night
And haply the Queen moon is on her throne,
Clustered around by all her starry fays;
But here there is no Light
Ode to a Nightingale

As we have mentioned earlier, this part of Saptagram was heavily forested. At a short distance from the village was a dense jungle. All by herself, Kapalkundala went there in search of the medicinal herb, following a narrow forest track. The night was exquisitely beautiful, utterly silent, devoid of the slightest sound. In the honey-sweet night sky, the moon rose silently above the scattered white clouds, spreading its tender glow; on earth, silently, the trees and vines of the forest rested in the cold moon-light; and in silence, the leaves on the trees reflected that moonlit glow. Amidst the vines and creepers, white flowers blossomed in silence. The birds and beasts were silent. Just occasionally, one could hear the wing-flaps of a bird disturbed in slumber; once in a while, the sound of a dry leaf falling, somewhere; at rare intervals, the slithering sound of a reptile's movement; and every now and then, the distant barking of dogs. Not that the air was still: the languorous spring breeze played upon the body. It was the faintest hint of a breeze, secret and silent, stirring only the outermost leaves on the trees; only the dark vine drooping to the earth was swayed by it; only the tiny fragments of cloud in the blue sky floated slowly in that breeze. Stirred by the same breeze, indistinct memories of former bliss awakened faintly in the heart.

Such memories were awakening in Kapalkundala's heart, as well; she remembered the moisture-laden vernal sea breeze, playing upon her long tresses as she stood on the sand dune's crest; gazing at the pure, limitless blue sky, she recalled the ocean, which mirrored that pure, endless blue. Lost in memories of the past, Kapalkundala proceeded on her way.

She walked on absent-mindedly, unmindful of where she was going and why. The path she had taken became gradually inaccessible; the forest thickened; the tangle of branches overhead blocked out the moonlight almost totally; the forest track was obscured from view. Unable to see the way, Kapalkundala came out of her reverie. Looking all around, she saw a light in the midst of this dense forest. Lutfunnissa, too, had seen the same light earlier. At such moments, Kapalkundala, by force of habit, was fearless, but curious. Advancing slowly towards the light, she found nobody at the spot where the fire was burning. But not far away was a broken building, invisible from a distance because the forest was so dense. The house, though brick-built, was a very small and humble abode, consisting of just one room. Human voices could be heard from within. With silent tread, Kapalkundala approached the house. As soon as she came near, she sensed that two persons were engaged in a cautious dialogue. At first, she understood nothing of what they said. Then, as her hearing grew sharper with concentrated effort, she overheard the following:

'To kill is my aim,' declared one. 'If you do not concur, I shall not help you. You, too, need not help me.'

'I am not a well-wisher, either,' replied the other. 'But lifelong exile for her is all I would agree to. I shall have no hand in a murder; rather, I would act to prevent it.'

'You are ignorant, and extremely foolish!' cried the first speaker. 'Let me apprise you of some facts. Listen to me carefully: I am about to narrate a deep secret. Go and check our surroundings first: I seem to hear the sound of human breathing.'

Kapalkundala had indeed positioned herself very close to the walls of the house, the better to hear their conversation. From acute anticipation combined with fear, her breath fell thick and fast.

At his companion's request, one of the men within the house stepped out, and immediately spotted Kapalkundala. In the bright moonlight, Kapalkundala also had a clear view of the man's approaching figure. She could not decide whether to be frightened, or overjoyed, at what she saw. She saw that he was dressed like a Brahmin in a simple dhoti, a shawl gracefully draped around his body. The Brahmin youth was of a very tender age, his countenance unlined. His face was exquisitely beautiful, as lovely as a woman's, but distinguished by a fiery arrogance not usually found in women. His hair was not trimmed by the barber's shearing-blade as was customary for men; like a woman's tresses, his uncut hair cascaded over his shawl, flowing in serpent-like coils down his back, shoulders, arms and chest. His forehead was broad, slightly distended, graced by a single visible vein at its centre. His eyes flashed like lightning. In his hand was a long, unsheathed sword. But his handsome image exuded a terrible aspect, as if some destructive desire had cast its shadow upon his golden complexion. His piercing glance, which seemed to probe the depths of her innermost being, struck terror into Kapalkundala's heart.

For a while, the two of them gazed at each other. Kapalkundala was the first to lower her eyes.

'Who are you?' asked the young man who had appeared on the scene.

If this question had been put to Kapalkundala a year earlier, amidst the keya forests of Hijli, she would have answered immediately, with composure. But now, having acquired some of the attitudes of a housewife, Kapalkundala could not reply at once. When she failed to respond, the stranger in Brahmin's attire addressed her severely.

'Kapalkundala!' he said. 'Why have you entered this dense forest at night?'

Hearing her name on the lips of a stranger in the night, Kapalkundala was startled, but also afraid. She could not reply immediately.

'Did you overhear our conversation?' demanded the stranger in Brahmin's attire, once again.

Suddenly, Kapalkundala found her tongue.

'I have the same query!' she declared, without answering his question. 'In this dense forest, so late at night, what conspiracy were the two of you hatching?'

For a while, the person in Brahmin's attire remained lost in thought, without offering any reply. A new means of attaining his ends seemed to have occurred to him. Grasping Kapalkundala's hand, he began to drag her away from the ruined building. Angrily, Kapalkundala snatched her hand away.

'What are you worried about?' whispered the one dressed as a Brahmin, in a very low voice, close to Kapalkundala's ear. 'I am not a man.'

Kapalkundala was even more amazed. These words restored some of her faith, but she was not completely convinced. She went along with the woman disguised as a Brahmin.

When they were out of sight of the ruined house, the Brahmin-impersonator whispered to Kapalkundala: 'Would you like to hear about our conspiracy? It was about you.'

'Yes I would!' cried Kapalkundala, her eagerness greatly heightened.

'Wait here, then, until I return.'

With these words, the woman in disguise returned to the ruined house. Kapalkundala waited at the same place for a while. But she was rather frightened at what she had seen and heard. Now, as she waited alone in the dark forest, her anxiety began to grow. Why this person in disguise had left her there to wait, who could tell? Perhaps she only wished to fulfil her evil intentions, now that an opportunity had presented itself. The Brahmin-impersonator was taking very long to return. Unable to wait any longer, Kapalkundala rose to her feet and started walking swiftly homewards.

The sky grew cloudy, dark as ink; even the faint light in the forest began to fade. Kapalkundala could delay no more. She began to run, emerging from the depths of the forest. As she ran, she seemed to hear footsteps behind her. But when she turned back to look, she could see nothing in the darkness. The Brahmin-impersonator was pursuing her, Kapalkundala told herself. Leaving the woods, she came out onto the narrow forest track described earlier. It was not so dark there; one could detect a human being within one's range of vision. But no one could be seen. She ran on. But again, very distinctly, she heard the sound of footsteps. The sky, full of inky clouds, grew even more threatening. Kapalkundala ran faster. Home was not far away, but she was barely within close range of it when a tremendous thunderstorm rent the skies with a fearsome sound.

Kapalkundala raced ahead. The person behind her was running hard, too, by the sound of it. Before the house came into view, the terrible storm broke over Kapalkundala's head. The clouds rumbled, accompanied by frequent bolts of thunder. Lightning flashed, again and again. The rain came down in torrents. Somehow managing to shield herself, Kapalkundala reached home. Crossing the courtyard, she entered her room. The door had been left open for her. She turned, facing the courtyard, to shut the door. She felt she saw a tall male figure standing in the courtyard. There was a flash of lightning. In that single flash, she recognised the man: he was the kapalik who lived on the shores of the sea.

In the World of Dreams

I had a dream, which was not all a dream.
Darkness

Slowly, Kapalkundala closed the door. Slowly, she entered the bedchamber, and slowly lay down on the bed. The human heart is a boundless ocean; when the wild winds rage, who can count the chain of waves they produce? Who could count the waves that surged in the ocean of Kapalkundala's heart?

That night, Nabokumar was too distressed to visit the antahpur, the private women's quarters of his house. Kapalkundala went to bed alone, but she could not sleep. All around her, even in the dark, she saw that countenance, framed in coils of windswept, rain-drenched hair. Kapalkundala began to relive the events of the past. She was reminded of her behaviour towards the kapalik at the time when she had deserted him; the monstrous deeds committed by the kapalik in the depths of the forest: his worship of the goddess Bhairavi, the way he had taken

Nabokumar captive, she remembered all those things. Kapal-kundala shuddered. She also recalled the events of the present night: Shyama's desire for the medicinal herb, Nabokumar's admonition, Kapalkundala's own heated rejoinder, and after-wards, the moonlit beauty of the forest, the darkness of the woods, the fellow-wanderer she had encountered in the forest, and the terrifying beauty of the stranger's appearance.

As dawn broke in all its glory, Kapalkundala dozed off. In that light slumber, she began to dream. She seemed to be adrift on a boat in the ocean's bosom, the same ocean she had seen before. The boat was beautifully decorated with bright yellow pennants; the oarsmen, bedecked with garlands, sang erotic songs about Radha and Shyam. From the western sky, the sun rained down a shower of gold. The ocean rejoiced in its glow; in the skies, the frolicking clouds bathed in it. Suddenly, it grew dark; the sun was nowhere to be seen. All the golden clouds had vanished. Heavy, inky clouds covered the entire sky. It was no longer possible to figure out directions at sea. The sailors turned the boat back, but could not decide which way to go. They ceased their music, and tore the garlands off their necks. The bright yellow pennants slipped down and fell into the ocean of their own accord. The wind rose; waves, high as trees, reared their heads; arising from the waves, the giant figure of a man with coiling locks lifted Kapalkundala's boat in his left hand, and made as if to cast it into the sea. At this juncture the awe-inspiring Brahmin-impersonator appeared, and took hold of the boat.

'Should I save you, or drown you?' he asked.

'Drown me!' said Kapalkundala suddenly.

The Brahmin-impersonator relinquished the boat. Now, the boat, too, acquired a voice.

'I can bear this burden no longer!' it declared. 'Let me enter the netherworld.'

With these words, the boat cast her into the waters and descended into the netherworld.

Bathed in sweat, Kapalkundala awakened from her dream and opened her eyes. She saw that it was dawn. Through the open window, the spring breeze wafted in; birds were singing in the gently swaying boughs of trees. Over the window hung some beautiful wild vines, laden with fragrant flowers. In her womanly way, Kapalkundala began to arrange the vines tidily. As she bound them together, she found a letter amidst the vines. Kapalkundala had been trained by the temple priest; she knew how to read. She read the following:

Tonight, after sundown, you must meet the Brahmin youth. You will learn of the urgent matters concerning yourself, which you wanted to know. I am the one disguised as a Brahmin.

Hints and Signals

I will have grounds
More relative than this.
Hamlet

All day, until sunset, Kapalkundala tried single-mindedly to determine whether or not it was advisable for her to meet the Brahmin-impersonator. Her hesitation did not arise from the belief that it was improper for a devoted young wife to meet a strange man alone, at night. She was sure that such a meeting was harmless, unless intended for a wrongful purpose. Just as persons of the same sex had the right to meet each other, so also, she felt, should persons of the opposite sexes enjoy the mutual right to intermingle. As it was also doubtful whether the Brahmin-impersonator was a man, such inhibitions were redundant. All the same, Kapalkundala hesitated for a long time, uncertain whether the outcome of such a meeting would be good or evil. First, the words uttered by the Brahmin-impersonator, then her vision of the kapalik, and afterwards, her dream: all these factors had aroused in her heart a strong apprehension that some evil fate awaited her in the near future. It did not seem far-fetched, moreover, to suspect that this impending doom was linked to the kapalik's arrival. Since this Brahmin-impersonator seemed to be the kapalik's accomplice, Kapalkundala's rendezvous with him could help that evil destiny to materialise, bringing about her downfall. After all, the Brahmin-impersonator had made it perfectly clear that Kapalkundala herself had been the subject of their conspiracy. But it was also possible that, at their meeting, he might announce his repudiation of that plot. The young Brahmin had been secretly conferring with another person, probably the kapalik. Their conversation had indicated the decision to do away with someone, or to banish someone to permanent exile, at the very least. Whose fate had they been discussing? The Brahmin-impersonator had clearly stated, after all, that Kapalkundala herself was the target of their evil conspiracy. So, it was her death or eternal banishment that they were plotting. What of that? And then there was the dream – what did it signify? In her dream, the Brahmin-impersonator had come to her aid at a time of great trouble; the same seemed to be proving true in practice. The Brahmin-impersonator wanted to reveal the entire truth to her. 'Drown her!' he had said, in the dream. Would he say the same in reality, as well? No, no – the goddess Bhavani, so benevolent to her devotees, had tried to protect Kapalkundala by offering her guidance in the form of a dream, implying that the Brahmin-impersonator wanted to come to her rescue:

if Kapalkundala rejected his help, she would drown. Kapalkundala therefore decided to meet him, after all. It is doubtful if a wise person would have arrived at such a decision; but the decisions of wise men are not our concern. Not being particularly wise, Kapalkundala did not arrive at a wise decision. Hers was the decision of a woman overwhelmed by curiosity, a young woman craving the sight of an awesomely attractive man, a woman who enjoyed nocturnal wanderings because she had been reared by a hermit, a woman held captive by her devotion to the goddess Bhavani. It was the decision of an insect about to plunge into the flames of a burning fire.

When it was dark, Kapalkundala, having completed some domestic chores, headed for the forest, as before. Before setting out, she turned up the flame of the lamp in her bedroom. As soon as she left the room, the light went out.

On her way, Kapalkundala realised she had forgotten something. Where had the Brahmin-impersonator asked her to meet him? She must re-read his letter. Returning to the house, she searched for the letter, but it was not where she had left it. She recalled having placed the letter in her hair-knot while braiding her hair, in order to carry it with her. She probed within her hair-knot, searching for the letter. When her fingers did not feel the letter, she loosened her hair-knot, but still, the letter was not to be found. Then she looked for it elsewhere in the house. Unable to find it anywhere, she finally decided that their rendezvous would probably be at their former meeting place. Once more, she set forth. Due to lack of time, she had not been able to re-braid those voluminous tresses. So, tonight, Kapalkundala proceeded on her way, framed by the mass of her unbound hair, as in the days of her adolescence.

On the Threshold

Stand you a while apart,
Confine yourself but in a patient list.
Othello

Just before dusk, while Kapalkundala was busy with her domestic chores, the letter had slipped out of her hair-knot and fallen to the ground, without her knowledge. It had caught Nabokumar's eye. He was surprised to see a letter fall out of her hair-knot. When Kapalkundala moved away to attend to another task, he picked up the letter, carried it outdoors, and read it. The contents of the letter could only lead to one conclusion. 'You will learn of the urgent matters concerning yourself, which you wanted to know.' What were the urgent matters she wanted to know about? Matters of the heart? Was the person in Brahmin's attire Mrinmayi's paramour? To someone who did not know what had transpired the previous night, no other conclusion could suggest itself.

When a devoted wife wishing to join her husband in death – or any other living person, impelled by some other motive – ascends the funeral pyre and sets it alight, he or she is at first encircled by a thick cloud of smoke. The smoke obscures one's vision; the world grows dark. Later, as the logs begin to burn, a few flames reach upwards, like serpent tongues, to lick the body here and there. Then, roaring flames envelop the entire body. Ultimately, with an explosive noise, the fire lights up the sky, soaring above one's head and reducing the body to a heap of ashes.

Such was Nabokumar's mental state upon reading the letter. At first, he was mystified; then he was assailed by doubt, followed by certainty, and ultimately, agony. The human heart cannot cope immediately with an excess of pain or joy; it can only accept such emotions gradually. Nabokumar was first encircled by a cloud of smoke; then, flames began to scorch his heart, and finally, the fire began to consume his heart, burning it to ashes. Prior to this, Nabokumar had already noticed that Kapalkundala disobeyed him in some matters. He had noted, in particular, that she would go alone, whenever and wherever she wished, even when he forbade her. She mingled freely with all and sundry, would roam alone in the woods at night, ignoring his injunctions. This would have made another person suspicious; but, knowing that to entertain doubts about Kapalkundala would be like the scorpion's fatal bite, Nabokumar had never harboured any suspicions for a single day. Today, too, he would not have allowed doubt to prevail, but this time he was confronted, not with suspicion, but with concrete fact.

When the first surge of agony had subsided, Nabokumar wept in silence for a long while, finding some consolation in his tears. Then, he resolutely decided upon his course of action. Tonight, he would say nothing to Kapalkundala, but when she made for the woods at dusk, he would follow her secretly. Having witnessed her utterly sinful behaviour, he would end his life. Rather than admonish Kapalkundala, he would take his own life instead. What else could he do? He would not have the strength to bear the burden of such a life.

Having come to this decision, he fixed his gaze upon the rear exit of the house, awaiting Kapalkundala's departure. After she had emerged, and walked some distance, Nabokumar also prepared to step out. But seeing her return for the letter, he moved out of sight. Once Kapalkundala had re-emerged and travelled a short distance, Nabokumar was again about to follow her, when he saw a tall male figure blocking the doorway. Who the person was, why he was standing there, Nabokumar had not the slightest wish to know. Even when he saw the man, he failed to notice him, anxious only to keep Kapalkundala in view. He placed his hand on the stranger's chest, to push him aside; but he could not make the man budge.

'Who are you?' demanded Nabokumar. 'Move aside – let me go!'

'Don't you know who I am?' The stranger's voice assailed the ears like the roar of the ocean. Nabokumar looked at him, and recognised the same kapalik he had encountered before, the ascetic with his tangled coils of hair.

Nabokumar started, but was not afraid. Suddenly, his face brightened.

'Is it you Kapalkundala is going to meet?' he wanted to know.

'No,' replied the kapalik.

The lamp of hope extinguished as soon as it had been ignited, Nabokumar's countenance clouded over, as before.

'Let me go, then!' he demanded.

'I'll let you go,' the kapalik answered, 'but there is something I must tell you. Hear me first.'

'What could you have to say to me?' Nabokumar protested. 'Have you come here to destroy my life, again? You may take my life; this time, I shall offer no resistance. Wait here; I shall be back soon. Why did I not sacrifice myself to please the gods? Now I have paid the price, ruined by the very person who had rescued me. Kapalik! Don't mistrust me this time. I shall return forthwith to surrender my life to you.'

'I have not come with the intention of killing you,' the kapalik informed him. 'That is not the wish of goddess Bhavani. The task I have come here to accomplish will meet with your approval. Come inside, and listen to what I have to say.'

'Not now!' declared Nabokumar. 'I shall listen to you after some time; for the moment, you must wait. I have an urgent task to perform; as soon as it is accomplished, I shall return.'

'My son, I know everything!' exclaimed the kapalik. 'You will follow the sinful woman. I know where she will go: I shall take you there, and show you what you want to see. Now, listen to me. Have no fear.'

'I have nothing to fear from you now,' Nabokumar told him. 'Come with me.'

With these words, Nabokumar escorted the kapalik into the house, offered him a floor-mat, and took his place beside him.

'Tell me what you have to say,' he demanded.

Re-encounter

Proceed there, and your divine task accomplish.
Kumarasambhava

Having taken his place on the floor-mat, the kapalik held out his arms for Nabokumar to view. Nabokumar saw that both his arms were broken.

The esteemed reader may recall that, on the night when Kapalkundala and Nabokumar had escaped from the seashore, the kapalik, while hunting for them, had fallen off the crest of a sand dune. Falling, he had tried to land on his arms in order to protect his body from injury; this saved his body, indeed, but he fractured both his arms. Narrating the entire episode to Nabokumar, the kapalik told him:

'I don't have much difficulty in performing my daily tasks. But there's no strength left in these arms of mine. In fact, it is difficult even to collect firewood.'

'Not that I realised instantly that my fall had broken my arms, leaving the rest of my body intact,' he continued. 'As soon as I fell, I fainted. At first, I remained unconscious for a stretch of time. Then, I drifted in and out of consciousness. How long I continued in this state, I cannot say. For two nights and a day, perhaps. Dawn was breaking when I completely regained consciousness. Just before that, I had been dreaming. As if the goddess Bhavani...' As he spoke, the kapalik's hair stood on end. 'As if the goddess Bhavani had appeared before my eyes. Frowning in anger, she admonished me: "O evil one, it is your impurity of mind that has disrupted your worship of me in this manner. Having fallen prey to your sensual desires, you have not yet offered up this maiden's blood to me. Because of this maiden, all the fruits of your previous spiritual labour have been destroyed. I shall never again accept your prayers!" When I fell weeping at her feet upon hearing her words, she was pleased. "My good man! I shall decree the only possible penance for this sin. You must sacrifice the very same Kapalkundala to me. Until you accomplish this task, don't offer me any prayers."'

'How long I took to recover, and by what means, I need not recount here. Eventually, having regained my health, I began my efforts to obey the goddess' decree. I found that my arms lacked even the strength of an infant. Without the physical power of my arms, my efforts would be futile. An accomplice was therefore necessary. But in matters of religion, human beings are narrow-minded. In this depraved age called Kaliyuga, this sinful era of Yavana rule, nobody is willing to act as an accomplice in such an undertaking. After much searching, I have managed to locate the sinful woman's abode. But lacking strength in my arms, I have not been able to carry out Bhavani's decree. I can only continue my tantrik prayer rituals, to accomplish my purpose. Last night, I was performing the fire ritual in the forest nearby, when with my own eyes I witnessed Kapalkundala's tryst with a Brahmin youth. Tonight, as well, she is on her way to meet him. If you wish to observe the scene, come with me, and I will show you.

'My son! Kapalkundala deserves to be sacrificed; I shall destroy her, as Bhavani has decreed. Kapalkundala has betrayed you, too; she deserves death at your hands, as well. So, give me the help I need. Capture this unfaithful woman; let us take her to the place of sacrifice. There, destroy her with your own hands. This will earn me forgiveness for my offence against the deity; your holy deed will earn you immortal virtue for your afterlife; the treacherous woman will be punished; it will be the ultimate revenge.'

The kapalik ended his speech. Nabokumar did not reply.

'My son!' urged the kapalik, seeing that he was silent. 'Now come and witness the scene I had promised to show you.'

Bathed in sweat, Nabokumar accompanied the kapalik.

In Conversation with the Co-wife

Be at peace; it is your sister that addresses you. Requite Lucretia's love.
Lucretia

Emerging from her house, Kapalkundala entered the forest. She went first to the ruined hut, where she met the Brahmin. Had it been daylight, she would have noticed that his countenance had lost much of its brightness.

'It is not advisable to say anything here, for the kapalik might arrive,' the Brahmin-impersonator told Kapalkundala. 'Let's go somewhere else.'

In the midst of the forest was a small clearing, with a path leading away from it. There the Brahmin-impersonator led Kapalkundala.

'Let me introduce myself first,' he said, once both of them were seated. 'You can judge for yourself how far to trust my words. En route from Hijali, travelling with your husband, you had encountered a Muslim woman one night. Do you recall the incident?'

'Was she the one who gave me her jewellery?'

'I am she!' declared the Brahmin-impersonator.

Kapalkundala was stunned.

'I have something even more amazing to reveal,' Lutfunnissa informed her. 'I am your co-wife!'

'Really!' cried Kapalkundala, astounded.

Lutfunnissa began to recount the story of her past. She spoke of her marriage, conversion, how she was rejected by her husband, of Dhaka, Agra, Jehangir, Mehrunnissa, her departure from Agra and residence in Saptagram, her encounter with Nabokumar, his behaviour towards her, her arrival in the woods in disguise the previous day, her meeting with the performer of the fire ritual – she narrated everything.

'Why did you wish to visit our house in disguise?' asked Kapalkundala at this point.

'To bring about your eternal separation from your husband,' replied Lutfunnissa.

Kapalkundala pondered over this. 'How would you have accomplished that?' she wanted to know.

'To begin with, I would have made your husband doubt your chastity. But what use talking of such things now? I have abandoned that plan. Now, if you do as I say, I can fulfil my aim through you; and yet, it will be for your own benefit.'

'Whose name did you hear from the person who was performing the fire ritual?'

'Your own name. To gauge whether he was praying for your harm or benefit, I touched his feet in obeisance, and waited by his side. There I remained, until his ritual was complete. Then, I asked him why he was offering prayers in your name. After speaking to him for a while, I realised that he had performed the ritual with malignant intent towards you. My needs were the same. When I confided this to him, we immediately decided to assist each other. He took me into the ruined house for a special consultation. There, he revealed his plan to me. It was your death he desired, but I had no such aim in mind. I have led a sinful life, but in taking the path of moral degradation, I have not fallen so low as to will the death of an innocent young girl. I refused to consent to his plan. At this juncture, you appeared on the scene. I think you may have overheard something.'

'Indeed, I overheard an argument of the kind you have described.'

'Taking me for an ignorant fool, that man wanted to offer me some advice. I left you concealed in the woods to go and listen to his intended plan, so as to brief you accordingly.'

'Then why didn't you come back?'

'He spoke at length; it took a long time to hear his extended narrative. You know that man particularly well. Can you guess who he is?'

'The kapalik, my former foster parent!'

'Indeed, it is he. First, the kapalik acquainted me with the facts: how you were found on the seashore, how he brought you up in that place, the arrival of Nabokumar, your escape with him. He also described all that had happened after your departure. You don't know about all those developments. I shall give you a detailed account, so that you know what transpired.'

Lutfunnissa proceeded to tell her about the kapalik's fall from the sand dune crest, the injury to his arms, and his dream. Hearing about the dream, Kapalkundala started, and trembled, agitated as if lightning had struck her heart.

'The kapalik has firmly resolved to follow the dictum of Bhavani,' continued Lutfunnissa. 'Because his arms have lost their strength, he desperately needs someone to help him. Taking me for the son of a Brahmin, he told me the entire story in the hope of making me his accomplice. Until now, I have not agreed to join him in this evil enterprise. I cannot vouch for my fickle heart, but I hope that I shall never consent to his plan. Rather, it is my intention to resist his resolve; that is why I have arranged this rendezvous with you. But I have not taken this step for purely unselfish motives. I am offering to save your life, but you must do something for me in return.'

'What can I do for you?' Kapalkundala wondered.

'Save my life, as well. Leave your husband.'

For a long time, Kapalkundala said nothing.

'Where should I go, once I have left my husband?'

'To other lands, far away. I shall give you a mansion to live in, wealth, an army of servants; you shall live like a queen.'

Once again, Kapalkundala fell into contemplation. In her mind's eye she scanned the whole world, but could see nobody who mattered. She looked within her own heart, but there, too, she found nobody, not even Nabokumar. Then why should she block the path to Lutfunnissa's happiness?

'Whether you have done me any good, I still cannot determine,' she told Lutfunnissa. 'I do not need a mansion, or wealth, or an army of servants. Why should I obstruct the path to your happiness? May your desire be fulfilled! From tomorrow, you will hear no tidings of the woman who stood in your way. I was once a wanderer in the wilds. To the wilds, as a wanderer, I shall return again.'

Lutfunnissa was wonderstruck; she had not hoped for such swift compliance.

'My sister!' she cried. 'May you live forever, for you have just granted me the boon of life! But only on one condition shall I let you go: tomorrow, at dawn, I'll send you a trusted, intelligent maidservant. Go with her. There is a woman of eminence in Burdhwan, a close friend of mine. She will look after all your needs.'

So intent were Lutfunnissa and Kapalkundala on their conversation, that they remained oblivious to immediate dangers. They failed to detect the hostile gaze of the kapalik and Nabokumar, who stood at the end of the forest path leading away from the clearing in which the two women had taken refuge.

Nabokumar and the kapalik were watching them, but unfortunately, from such a distance, they could hear nothing of their conversation. Had the range of human hearing matched the scope of human sight, who can tell whether the tide of human sorrow would have risen or declined? Creation is so exquisitely complicated! Nabokumar observed that Kapalkundala's hair was unbound, flowing free. In the days before she became his, she used to leave her hair unbraided. Again, he noticed that her heavy tresses had cascaded down to the young Brahmin's back, to mingle with his shoulder-length locks. So massive was the weight of Kapalkundala's hair, and so closely did they lean towards each other as they conducted their whispered conversation, that Kapalkundala's locks had fallen across Lutfunnissa's back. The two women had not noticed it. But the sight caused Nabokumar to slowly sink to the ground.

Seeing this, the kapalik produced a coconut shell from his waistband. 'My son!' he urged. 'You are losing your valour. Drink this sacred potion, blessed by Bhavani. It will revive you.'

The kapalik held the container to Nabokumar's lips. Absent-mindedly, he drank from it to quench his acute thirst. Nabokumar was not aware that this delicious fluid was extraordinarily potent liquor, brewed by the kapalik himself. Drinking it, he at once felt stronger.

Meanwhile, Lutfunnissa continued to address Kapalkundala in a low voice, as before: 'My sister! It is beyond my power to repay you for what you have done. Still, if you remember me always, even that would make me happy. The jewellery I gave, you have donated in charity, I'm told. I have nothing on me at this moment. To take care of other needs that might arise tomorrow, I had carried a ring concealed in my hair, but by the

Lord's grace, I need no longer pursue that evil plan. Keep this ring. Wear it, and when you look at the ring, think of your sister, the Yavani. Tonight, if your husband wants to know where you got this ring, tell him that Lutfunnissa gave it to you.'

With these words, Lutfunnissa removed a jewel-encrusted ring from her finger, and handed it to Kapalkundala. This, too, was witnessed by Nabokumar. The kapalik, who had been supporting him, felt his body tremble again, and once more offered him liquor to drink. The spirit went to Nabokumar's head, and began to play havoc with his nature, uprooting even the tender seedling of affection.

Taking her leave of Lutfunnissa, Kapalkundala headed back for her own home. By the secret path that Lutfunnissa had taken, Nabokumar and the kapalik began to trail Kapalkundala.

On the Way Home

No spectre greets me – no vain shadow this.
Laodamia

Slowly, Kapalkundala walked homewards. Very slowly she walked, with a gentle tread, for she was lost in deep thought. Lutfunnissa's words had utterly transformed Kapalkundala's frame of mind. She was ready to sacrifice her life. Sacrifice her life, for whom? For Lutfunnissa? It was not so.

In matters of the heart, Kapalkundala was the child of a tantrik. Just as a tantrik does not hesitate to kill others in the hope of earning goddess Kali's blessings, so was Kapalkundala ready to sacrifice her own life to fulfil the same desire. Not that Kapalkundala had shared the kapalik's single-minded pursuit of shakti, the divine gift of spiritual power. All the same, exposed day and night to the sight, sound and practice of shakti worship, she had developed in her heart a special devotion to Kali. She was strongly convinced that Bhairavi was ruler of the created world, as well as its liberator. Her compassionate heart could not bear to see the place for Kali worship flooded with human blood, but in all other respects, she spared no effort to express her devotion. Now, the same Bhairavi, ruler of the universe, arbiter of human joys and sorrows, liberator of the soul, had appeared in a dream to decree that Kapalkundala should surrender her life. Why should Kapalkundala not obey that decree?

You and I don't wish to die. Whatever we may say in moments of anger, this world is full of happiness. It is the hope of finding happiness, and not in search of sorrow, that we spin around the world like a ball on a playground. If ever, as a consequence of our own misdeeds, that hope is frustrated, we at once break into loud protests about our sorrows. Sorrow is therefore not a law of life, but a deviation from the normal and customary. For you and me, there is happiness everywhere. For the sake of happiness, we remain rooted in this world, not wishing to relinquish it. But love is the primary strand in the ties that bind us to life. Kapalkundala did not have such ties – she had no ties at all. So, there was no holding her back.

A person without any ties proceeds with unchecked speed. When the waterfall descends from the mountain crest, who can restrain its flow? If Kapalkundala's heart grew restless, who could restore her tranquillity? When a young elephant is in heat, who can calm it down?

'Why should I not surrender this body at the goddess Jagadiswari's feet?' Kapalkundala asked herself. 'Of what use are the five senses to me?'

She asked herself these questions, but was unable to arrive at any definite answers. Even in the absence of all other worldly ties, the senses bind one to life.

Kapalkundala walked on with lowered head. When the heart is overcome with some monstrous emotion, this single obsession makes one oblivious to external surroundings. In this state, even insubstantial things seem to take on a material shape. Such was Kapalkundala's condition at this time.

'My child!' she seemed to hear a voice call out, from above. 'I shall show you the way.'

Startled, Kapalkundala looked up. Etched in the clouds that had just formed in the sky, she saw what looked like the outline of a figure. A stream of blood flowed from the garland of human skulls around the neck of this apparition; encircling her waist was a girdle of human arms; in her left hand was a human skull; rivulets of blood streamed down her body; and adorning her forehead, at the outer edge of her extraordinarily bright, fiery eye, hung the crescent moon! Right arm upraised, Bhairavi seemed to beckon to Kapalkundala.

Gazing skywards, Kapalkundala went on her way. Before her, leading the way, that figure, resembling a newly formed mass of clouds, moved across the pathways of the sky. Sometimes the shape of the apparition, with her garland of skulls, was hidden by clouds; sometimes, it was clearly visible to the eye. Gazing at her, Kapalkundala walked on.

Nabokumar and the kapalik had not seen the apparition. Fuelled by alcohol, Nabokumar's heart was on fire.

'Kapalik!' he exclaimed to his companion, losing patience at the slowness of Kapalkundala's tread.

'What is it?'

'Give me something to drink!' he demanded, in Sanskrit.

Once again, the kapalik offered him liquor.

'Why wait any longer?' asked Nabokumar.

'Why wait?' the kapalik repeated.

'Kapalkundala!' roared Nabokumar, in a booming voice.

The sound of his voice startled Kapalkundala. Of late, nobody had addressed her by that name. She turned around. Nabokumar and the kapalik came up, to stand face to face with her. At first, Kapalkundala could not recognise them.

'Who are you?' she asked. 'Are you messengers from hell?'

The next instant, she recognised them. 'No, no, you are my Father!' she exclaimed. 'Have you come to offer me up in sacrifice?'

Nabokumar took hold of her arm, with a grip of iron.

'Come with us, my child!' invited the kapalik, in tender, honeyed tones.

With these words, he headed for the cremation grounds, leading the way.

Kapalkundala glanced up, in the direction where she had seen the terrible figure of the goddess who ranged the sky. She saw the goddess burst into peals of laughter, pointing with a long trident at the path taken by the kapalik. Wordlessly, like one blind to her fate, Kapalkundala followed the kapalik. Gripping her arm tightly as before, Nabokumar walked on.

In the Land of Spirits

In her collapse, she brought her husband down, as well,
As the oil, when it drips from the lamp, brings the flame
   down, too.
Raghuvamsha

The moon sank beneath the horizon. The universe was plunged into darkness. The kapalik led Kapalkundala to his place of worship. It was a wide stretch of sand on the shores of the Ganga. Facing it was an even larger stretch of sand, the cremation ground. At high tide, an expanse of shallow water separated the two sandy tracts; at low tide, the wet area disappeared. At this time, the space was free of water. The part of the cremation ground facing the Ganga was far above the river. To enter the river at that point would mean plunging from a height, straight into deep waters. The sandy shore, moreover, had been eroded by the continuous assault of waves cast ashore by the relentless breeze. From time to time, a chunk of earth would break off, crashing down into the bottomless waters.

There was no lamp at the place of worship, only a flaming torch. By its light, the cremation ground, indistinctly seen, appeared even more monstrous. Arrangements had been made for prayers, the hom, or fire ceremony, and the ritual human sacrifice. The heart of the immense river stretched out in the dark. The Chaitra wind blew with unchecked force across the Ganga's breast; the sky resounded with the noise of crashing waves, whipped to turbulence by the wind. Every now and then, from the cremation ground, the hoarse call of scavenging beasts could be heard.

Having positioned Nabokumar and Kapalkundala on suitably arranged reed-mats, the kapalik began his devotional rites as prescribed by tantrik law. At the appropriate time, he instructed Nabokumar to take Kapalkundala for a ritual bath. Taking her by the hand, Nabokumar led Kapalkundala across the cremation ground. Bones pierced the soles of their feet. A water-filled funeral pitcher cracked under Nabokumar's foot when he trod on it. Close to it lay the corpse of an unfortunate wretch for whom nobody had performed the last rites. Their feet touched the corpse. Kapalkundala walked around it, while Nabokumar stepped on it as he proceeded on his way. Circling the area, the scavenging animals called out loudly at the approach of the two humans; some advanced to attack them, others retreated with a noisy tread. Nabokumar's hand was trembling, Kapalkundala discovered; but she herself was fearless and steady.

'Are you afraid?' she asked him.

Nabokumar's intoxication was waning.

'Afraid, Mrinmayi?' he replied, very gravely. 'No, that is not the reason.'

'Then why do you tremble?'

Only a woman's voice can capture the tone in which she asked this question. Only a woman who melts in compassion can speak in such a tone. Who would have expected such a tone of voice from Kapalkundala here, at the cremation ground, when her own death was imminent?

'It is not fear,' asserted Nabokumar. 'I tremble in rage because I am unable to weep.'

'Why should you weep?'

Once more, the same tone of voice.

'Why should I weep? What would you know, Mrinmayi! After all, the sight of beauty has never driven you mad…' As he spoke, Nabokumar's voice choked with agony. 'You have never come to the cremation ground to tear out your own heart and throw it away.'

Suddenly, Nabokumar burst into a loud wail, and flung himself at Kapalkundala's feet.

'Mrinmayi! O Kapalkundala! Save me! I fall at your feet. Tell me, just once, that you are not unfaithful! Say it just once, and I shall clasp you to my heart and carry you home.'

Kapalkundala took Nabokumar by the hand and helped him to his feet.

'You never asked me about it,' she reminded him gently.

As they spoke, the two of them had reached the water's edge. Kapalkundala was ahead, standing with her back to the river, just a step away from the water. The tide was rising; Kapalkundala was standing on the brink, at the edge of the river's vertical bank.

'You never asked me,' she said.

'I have lost my senses – what am I to ask you?' cried Nabokumar, like one driven insane. 'Tell me, Mrinmayi, tell me, tell me, tell me! Accept me. Come home with me!'

'I shall answer your question. The person you saw tonight is Padmavati. I have not been unfaithful. I tell you this by way of information. But I shall not return home again. I have come here to surrender this body at goddess Bhavani's feet; I shall fulfil my resolve. You must go home. I go to my death. Don't even grieve for me.'

'No, Mrinmayi! No!' With a loud cry, Nabokumar stretched out his arms to clasp Kapalkundala to his breast. He could not find her anymore. Spurred by the Chaitra wind, an enormous wave crashed upon the shore, where Kapalkundala had been standing. Instantly, with a deafening crash, the chunk of earth fell into the river current, carrying Kapalkundala with it. Nabokumar heard the sound of the collapsing landmass, and saw Kapalkundala vanish. At once, he plunged into the water. He was not a bad swimmer. For a while, he swam about, searching for Kapalkundala. He did not find her, nor did he emerge from the water.

In the river's endless flow, tossed about by the waves surging in the stormy winds of spring, where did Kapalkundala and Nabokumar disappear?

Glossary

Kumkum: Powder used for social or religious markings in Hinduism
Paan: Tradition consisting of chewing betel leaf combined with spices
    and areca nut held together with a clove; chewed as a palate cleanser
    and breath-freshener offered to guests as a sign of hospitality
Pir: Spiritual guide, honorific denoting possession of power
Subedar: Provincial governor

Biographical note

Bankim Chandra Chatterjee was born in Kanthalpara in 1838, the youngest of three sons, and was educated at the Mohsin College in Hooghly and later at the Presidency College from which he graduated in 1857. Chatterjee was married at the age of eleven; his wife was five years old and was to die when he was twenty-two. His second wife, Rajalakshmi Devi, bore him three daughters.

He was appointed Deputy Collector of Jessore and then became Deputy Magistrate, during which time he also completed a law degree. He was made a Companion, Order of the Indian Empire, in 1894.

Most famous as the author of *Bande Mataram*, now the National Song of India, Chatterjee is a key figure in Bengali literature, writing novels and essays. Having begun his literary career by writing verse, Chatterjee changed swiftly to fiction. *Rajmohan's Wife*, written in English, was Chatterjee's first novel to appear in print. His first romance in Bengali, *Durgeshnandini*, was published in 1865. Later romances were set in a larger historical context, part of Chatterjee's move towards writing works on intellectual matters for Bengali speakers, a factor which played a part in bringing about a veritable Bengali cultural renaissance. He wrote in all fourteen novels and a large number of literary essays and treatises.

In April 1872, the author began publishing a monthly literary magazine named *Bangadarshan*, the first edition of which he filled mostly with his own work. The magazine was to include novels, essays, literary criticism and religious discussion.

Chatterjee died in 1894, in Kolkata, and is now remembered not only as the father of modern Bengali literature but also as a key figurehead in the Indian nationalist struggle.

Radha Chakravarty was born in Kolkata and studied English Literature at Delhi University, where she now teaches the same subject at Gargi College. Her work includes translations of Tagore's *Boyhood Days* (Hesperus, 2011), *Chokher Bali*, *Gora*, *Farewell Song: Shesher Kabita* and *The Land of Cards: Stories, Poems and Plays* (translations of Tagore's writings for children). She has also translated Mahasweta Devi's *In the Name of the Mother* and *Crossings: Stories from Bangladesh and India* and the collection of stories *Vermillion Clouds: A century of women's stories from Bengal*. She is the co-editor of *The Essential Tagore* jointly published by Visva Bharati and Harvard University Press and *Writing Feminism: South Asian Voices* and *Writing Freedom: South Asian Voices*. Her academic publications include the book *Feminism and Contemporary Women Writers* as well as numerous essays and review articles.

HESPERUS PRESS

Hesperus Press is committed to bringing near what is far –
far both in space and time. Works written by the greatest
authors, and unjustly neglected or simply little known in
the English-speaking world, are made accessible through
new translations and a completely fresh editorial approach.
Through these classic works, the reader is introduced to the
greatest writers from all times and all cultures.

For more information on Hesperus Press, please visit our
website: **www.hesperuspress.com**

NEW AND FORTHCOMING TITLES
FROM HESPERUS WORLDWIDE

Author	Title	Foreword writer
Eduardo Belgrano Rawson	*Washing Dishes in Hotel Paradise*	
Buddhadeva Bose	*My Kind of Girl*	
Shiro Hamao	*The Devil's Disciple*	
Kanoko Okamoto	*A Riot of Goldfish*	David Mitchell
Rabindranath Tagore	*Boyhood Days*	Amartya Sen
Rabindranath Tagore	*Farewell Song*	

SELECTED TITLES FROM HESPERUS PRESS

Author	Title	Foreword writer
M. Ageyev	*A Romance with Cocaine*	Toby Young
Mary Borden	*The Forbidden Zone*	Malcolm Brown
Rupert Brooke	*Letters from America*	Benjamin Markovits
Anthony Burgess	*The Eve of St Venus*	
Ivy Compton-Burnett	*Pastors and Masters*	Sue Townsend
Walter de la Mare	*Missing*	Russell Hoban
E.M. Forster	*The Obelisk*	Amit Chaudhuri
Graham Greene	*No Man's Land*	David Lodge
L.P. Hartley	*The Brickfield*	
Aldous Huxley	*After the Fireworks*	Fay Weldon
Mikhail Kuzmin	*Wings*	Paul Bailey
Jack London	*The People of the Abyss*	Alexander Masters
Klaus Mann	*Alexander*	Jean Cocteau
Luigi Pirandello	*Loveless Love*	
Vita Sackville-West	*The Heir*	
Leonardo Sciascia	*A Simple Story*	Paul Bailey
Frank Wedekind	*Mine-Haha*	
Edith Wharton	*Fighting France: from Dunkerque to Belfort*	Colm Tóibín
Leonard Woolf	*A Tale Told by Moonlight*	Victoria Glendinning
Virginia Woolf	*Memoirs of a Novelist*	
Yevgeny Zamyatin	*We*	Alan Sillitoe